Exposed Desire

The Benedict Brothers

Tara Sue Me

Exposed Desire (The Benedict Brothers, Book 3)

Copyright © 2023 by Tara Sue Me, After Six Publishing

For more about this author, please visit www.tarasueme.com

This is a rewritten, revised, and reedited version of BROKEN PROMISE, which is no longer available.

Editing by The Pro Book Editor

Cover Design by 100covers.com

eBook ISBN: 9781950017492

Paperback ISBN: 9781950017508

Chapter One

Though he would deny it if asked, Kipling Benedict felt oddly out of place at his younger brother's vow renewal. He chalked it up to both of his younger brothers now being in committed relationships, but that didn't make him feel any better.

In fact, while he stood by Knox and listened as he pledged to love, honor, and cherish his wife, Bea, Kipling actually felt worse because he was envious of what his brothers had. He'd accepted a long time ago that his station in life was to be alone.

Falling in love hard and fast in college, only to discover it was his net worth the young woman had found attractive, had left him not wanting to try again. Being alone was so much easier.

However, at times such as this, he became acutely aware of the differences between acceptance and contentment. While he may have accepted he would be alone, he was not content.

"You may kiss your bride," the minister said, dragging him back to the small historic chapel Bea had selected for the renewal of their vows—vows celebrated by family and friends, as opposed to the first ones the couple had taken in a secret Vegas ceremony.

Kipling clapped as his brother took his wife in his arms and dipped her low, snagging a kiss while he did so. They both looked so blissfully in love that he couldn't help but smile at the joy and peace they exuded. If anyone deserved a happily ever after, it was Knox and Bea. They'd both narrowly escaped with their lives, months earlier, after a security guard who'd been hired to protect Bea turned out to be the thug who'd beaten her up and left her for dead.

Kipling had asked Knox a few days ago if he was ready to give up his bachelor status forever, since he was having a public wedding this time. They'd been outside. Tilly, the fiancée of his youngest brother, Keaton, sat at a nearby table in the garden with both Keaton and Bea. From the look of things, they were studying a map, trying to determine the best location for a public vegetable garden.

Knox had only replied, "The wedding won't come soon enough for me."

Kipling felt the truth in his words that day, but now he saw it as the happy couple stood and laughed, only having eyes for each other.

Kipling's mouth curled up into a smile as the couple walked down the aisle, nodding to the small gathering of friends and family in attendance. Then his hands froze when he saw who waited near the chapel doors.

Alyssa Adams.

Officer Alyssa Adams.

He lifted an eyebrow in a silent question, as he had not expected her to attend today. It was ridiculous how happy the sight of her left him, especially since she made no secret of the fact that she didn't like him, his money, or anything about him. She presented him with a challenge, and he never backed down from a challenge. But it was more than that. It was the way she never took any crap from him and how alive he felt after one of their verbal sparring sessions.

He kept his eyes on her as he made his way down the aisle behind his brother. Though he had seen her wear a dress once before at the party announcing Keaton and Tilly's engagement and the new division of Benedict Industries, today she wore a more formal one. It hit above her knee, showing off her long legs and toned calves. He'd always considered himself a leg man. Yes, breasts were great, and he had no problem appreciating a woman's backside, but legs... There was just something about a woman's legs. Especially when they looked like Alyssa's. Long and lean and strong. It was so easy to imagine them wrapped around his waist while he angled his hips to—

"Stop it." His youngest brother, Keaton, punched his arm. "Seriously, man. What happened to your poker face?"

They had made it out of the chapel and were waiting for the remaining guests to leave the church so they could all walk to the reception area.

"I don't know what you're talking about," Kipling told Keaton.

In truth, he shouldn't have been the least bit interested in the police officer. It seemed as if each time he saw her, she only gave him disturbing news about his family or, worse yet, arrested him. He didn't understand how he could possibly find her attractive, but he did. Not only that, but he wanted her. Badly.

"You don't know what I'm talking about." His youngest brother snorted. "Yeah, right."

Kipling shot him a look that would have stopped

another man in his tracks. A look that, apparently, didn't work on younger brothers. No, Keaton kept right on talking.

"You know," Keaton said, nodding toward Alyssa, who was currently chatting with Janie Roberts, her old partner and soon-to-be sister-in-law. "If you wanted, you could, I don't know, ask her out or something."

He thought about playing dumb, pretending he wasn't sure who Keaton was talking about, but he'd never been one to play the fool, and he sure as hell wasn't going to start now.

"It's not as simple as that," Kipling told his younger brother. It was a pat answer, but the truth. Looking at Alyssa while she spoke to her friend, he wished things were different.

Damn, but he could watch her for hours. Today, he saw very little of the straitlaced investigator she was around him, and he found the contrast mesmerizing. She talked with Janie using her entire body. The animated way she moved and her genuine smile held him captivated. Not to mention, he'd always seen her with her hair pulled back in a ponytail, but today she'd freed it to fall around her shoulders. The sunlight made the normal brown a plethora of colors: blonde, red, and even hints of black. He clenched his fists, wanting nothing more than to run his fingers through it to test the softness.

Keaton narrowed his eyes and crossed his arms. "Why isn't it that simple?"

"I'm not going to stand here and explain," Kipling said. "You're going to have to take me at my word."

"If this is about that girl in college..." Keaton started, but stopped at Kipling's raised hand.

"Don't go there," Kipling warned his younger brother. "Not now. Not ever."

He would live his life and never complain if no one ever brought up the girl he had dated in college. The one he had fallen hard for. The one he had planned to marry. The one who had made a fool out of him.

His stomach twisted, and he wondered if he'd ever be able to think of her without feeling the urge to throw up. He reminded himself that at least he'd gotten out of the situation and hadn't been stupid enough to elope. Over Christmas break, she'd asked if he wanted to stop by a courthouse before arriving at Benedict House.

Even then, it appeared as if Keaton was going to argue with him. Fortunately, Tilly came up to them and looped her arm through Keaton's.

"Come on, you guys," Tilly said. "The photographer wants to do some family shots."

"Why do I have to get my picture taken?" Kipling mumbled while straightening his tie. "It's not my wedding."

But he followed Keaton and Tilly to the front of the chapel anyway, unable to keep himself from looking over his shoulder at Alyssa one last time.

Chapter Two

"What's the deal with the oldest Benedict brother?" Janie asked Alyssa as the family moved off toward the photographer.

"What makes you think there's a deal?" Alyssa asked instead of answering.

Janie flashed her *I know what you're trying to do* smile. "If I was uncertain as to whether or not there was a deal, your answer proved its existence."

Alyssa should have known she couldn't fool Janie. They'd worked together and been friends for far too many years for Alyssa to think she could pull one over on her. It didn't matter that life would be a lot easier if there wasn't a deal with Kipling; the truth was there was something between the two of them.

More than likely, it was nothing but lust. He'd never tried to hide his appreciation for the way she looked. Even when she shot him down and told him off, inside it thrilled her. The bigger part of her loved that Kipling took notice of more than her mind. Few men did. And, sure, some small part of herself hated that she'd spent hours in front of the mirror today, trying to decide which dress he'd like. She'd told herself three hundred times she didn't care what he thought of her. But the look of pure animal magnetism he'd shot her as he walked out of the chapel? Worth. Every. Second.

She wasn't about to admit anything of the sort, though. Especially not when Janie wore a grin like a cat who just ate the world's biggest canary.

"The deal," Alyssa told her, "is that nothing can ever happen between us. I arrested the man, for crying out loud. Not to mention, it would be a horrible breach of ethics."

But Janie, of course, wasn't going to be defeated that easily. She put a hand on her hip. "You mean like what I did when I started dating Brent?"

That was why Alyssa didn't want to go down the Janie-and-Brent road. Janie had been working undercover at a local gentlemen's club as a bartender, looking into the unsolved mystery of several kidnapped women, many of whom eventually turned out to have been murdered. Janie met Brent there, but unfortunately, he was considered a suspect at the time, and her boss placed her on administrative leave after finding out they were involved. Janie felt strongly that Brent wasn't the man they were looking for. Even so, it was at great personal risk that she continued seeing him. Eventually, he was cleared by DNA evidence, but Janie was not able to leave the case alone and was fired when her boss caught her investigating.

"I would be remiss if I didn't point out you were, in fact, fired from that job," Alyssa said.

"True, but life has turned out so much better," Janie said without missing a beat. "No offense, but you couldn't pay me enough to work at the Charleston PD again."

Alyssa didn't doubt her statement at all. Brent had

asked Janie to move to Washington, DC, with him when he'd been offered a position in the capital city. The couple now lived in their DC penthouse for half the year and in his multimillion-dollar restored historical home along the Battery in Charleston for the remaining six. Not only that, but they were planning a wedding for the following May. Alyssa was getting ready to say something when Brent walked up.

"Ladies." He slid behind Janie and put his arms around her. "Pictures are over. Everyone's heading to the reception."

With the chapel being centrally located, it was much easier to leave the cars and walk to the reception venue, a nearby private ballroom. At the moment, Knox and Bea led the group, with the rest of the Benedict family following behind.

"Oh," Janie said. "There's Tilly. I didn't get to speak to her before the ceremony."

Janie and Tilly had become friends while working at the bar where Janie was undercover. Tilly was now engaged to Keaton Benedict. Honestly, it boggled Alyssa's brain sometimes how interconnected everyone seemed to be. Except her. She felt like an outsider. The cold, hard realization made her want to leave.

"I think I'll head home," Alyssa said.

"Why?" Janie asked.

"I was only invited because of you, and seriously, what's the point in going to the reception?" Leaving made perfect sense to her, but Janie shook her head.

"You're not getting out of it that easy," her friend said. "Come on. People will talk if you leave now."

"And we certainly can't have that," Alyssa mumbled, but she allowed herself to be led away.

An hour later, Alyssa was still trying to plan her escape. Staying had in no way made her feel any less of an outsider. Surely she'd been at the reception long enough to not cause offense if she left.

She let her gaze wander to where Kipling stood, talking with his brothers. Did he not have a date? She hadn't seen him with anyone. The more she thought about it, the odder it seemed. He was a good-looking and wealthy man. One with the reputation of a playboy with his choice of women to pick from and have stand by his side. Why would he show up alone at his brother's renewal ceremony?

Of course, he picked that moment to look around and caught her staring. She ducked her head and turned to watch Brent and Janie dancing. They were discussing something very intently but laughed every so often. If she had to guess, she'd bet the conversation was about their own wedding. The thought made her smile.

"Dance with me."

She jumped at the sound of Kipling behind her.

Without turning around, she replied, "No, that's okay. I'm fine." Because the thought of dancing—of being—*that* close to Kipling and having his arms around her made her skin heat.

"It wasn't a question."

She spun around to find him smiling and all but laughing. She decided to play along and raised an eyebrow. "Really? Don't you know it's not polite to go up and command a woman dance with you?"

The hint of a smile teased his lips. "I thought you knew me well enough to know I've never been considered polite."

She couldn't think of anything to say back, so she stood there, feeling flustered. Damn, Kipling Benedict. She should have left after the ceremony and not cared about being offensive.

He took a step closer. "I see you standing here, watching the couples dance, and yet you're not dancing. I realize you didn't come with a date, and I don't have a date." He shrugged. "We might as well have a go."

"No, thank you," she said. "I don't want to be anyone's pity dance."

"Let's get one thing straight, why don't we." He leaned down and spoke in a low voice she knew no one else heard. "I do very many things and I do them for all kinds of reasons, but I never do anything out of pity, especially when it comes to a beautiful woman."

Her brain threatened to short-circuit. Was he saying he thought she was beautiful? She blinked. "Why would you...?" She trailed off as his hand moved to stroke her shoulder.

"We've both tried to ignore it, to pretend it's not there, but we know better. There's something between us." His voice grew rougher. "Let's give into it for today. For one dance."

She let her gaze move to the dancing couples, imagining being in Kipling's arms and having him in hers. She stopped the yes on her lips before it had a chance to slip out. "It's not appropriate. I'm involved in several cases with ties to your family."

"It's one dance, Alyssa." He didn't move his hand from her shoulder. The touch of his fingers made her want to feel his hands everywhere. "We're at my brother's wedding. There's nothing wrong with two single people enjoying themselves."

Why did she get the impression he was talking about more than a dance?

She closed her eyes, but blocking her sight did nothing to diminish the way his touch felt. It would be so easy to get lost in his touch. She could do it without even thinking twice. Agreeing to a dance would be one step down a path filled with nothing but heartache and trouble.

"Yes," she said anyway.

His hand slipped off her shoulder, and he held it out to her. God, she was actually doing this. She took his offered hand, and their fingers entwined.

He led them to the dance floor without a word. She kept her gaze focused forward, not looking to either side for fear of seeing everyone's reaction. She didn't realize how stiff and uncomfortable she looked until he whispered, "It's not an execution, you know. A smile wouldn't be remiss."

She smiled, but it felt fake. What didn't feel fake was her body's reaction when he slipped his arms around her. She lowered her head, hoping to keep to herself how her skin flushed at such close contact with Kipling.

"If I'd known you would feel so good in my arms, I'd have asked you to dance long before now," he said.

She tried to imagine them dancing at any of the previous times they'd been together. The image of them dancing while she arrested him made her chuckle with its ridiculousness.

"There we go," Kipling said. "Now people will think we're having a good time instead of assuming I'm torturing you."

She pulled back to look at him and make a snappy comeback, but instead she found herself caught up in his eyes. They were the most mesmerizing color. A light brown that somehow appeared golden. How had she never noticed his eyes before, and why did they seem so familiar?

The corner of his mouth uplifted in a half smile. "Cat got your tongue?"

"What?"

"You looked like you were going to say something, but then you stopped."

Had she? "I don't remember."

"That's not good," he said. "I don't mind rendering you speechless, but affecting your mental capacity isn't on my agenda."

She'd like to know what *was* on his agenda concerning her. She bet it was mind-blowing. But what was truly mind-blowing was the way he looked at her with such intensity. It was a bit unnerving, and she was starting to understand why Kipling excelled in business. Very few people could stand up to the scrutiny of his gaze. Fortunately, she'd had plenty of experience dealing with intense stares.

"Why are you looking at me like that?" she asked.

"Like what?"

"Like you're looking for something or waiting for me to do something."

"Am I?" he asked in such a way that proved he was, in fact, the most tedious man ever.

His question didn't warrant a reply. She tried to focus on the blank walls, and willed the song to be over soon. Once it was, she could try to pretend his arms didn't feel as good as they did and that his body didn't seem *oh so right* pressed up against hers.

"Actually," he said, "I was wondering if you'd like to have dinner with me?"

She stopped dancing. "Are you asking me out? Seriously?"

"For someone who didn't want to cause a scene, you aren't being the most discreet at the moment."

She glanced around and saw quite a few eyes watching. She smiled at them and nodded to Kipling, and they began to dance once more.

"Why would you ask me out?" she said.

"You know, I didn't peg you as the type needing an ego boost, but you're smart and attractive."

The sincerity of his expression took her breath and she had to look away.

"And I'm willing to bet, underneath the layers of sarcasm, you have a delightful personality. I'd like to find out."

She wondered how much he'd had to drink. "I arrested you."

"And later released me."

"I have actively investigated your family."

"And you've found no evidence of anything shady," he said, obviously enjoying their exchange way too much.

"You're impossible."

"Now, I wouldn't say that. Difficult? Maybe. Challenging? Perhaps. But not impossible. Not for you."

Her body shivered at the way his voice lowered for the last three words. "I don't... I mean... It's not..." Why did this man leave her so flustered? "Not a good idea."

Thankfully, the end of the song saved her from having to say anything else. She pulled out of his embrace, turned, and walked away, ignoring his calls for her to stop.

Jade

I stood across the street from the reception, knowing anyone leaving could see me if they looked hard enough. It was the closest I'd been to any of the Benedicts in over a month, having only recently decided I'd tell Bea everything. Unfortunately, my delay meant more than likely I'd have to wait longer. Certainly Bea and the middle Benedict brother would be going somewhere for a honeymoon.

I wanted to bring King down, and to do that, I needed to convince the Benedicts to work with me. I'd talked with Keaton once, but that felt like so long ago. Based on my last trip to Benedict House, the best way to get to the brothers would be to go through Bea. If I had to wait, I'd wait.

The reception-hall doors opened, and I craned my head, trying to catch a glimpse of the bridal couple. I was so focused on the scene before me, I didn't hear the footsteps behind me until it was too late.

Strong arms came around me at the same time I inhaled the scent of evil. Then it spoke.

"I'm going to make you wish you never left."

I tried to struggle, but he held tight. Something sharp pricked my neck. Knox and Bea walked out of the reception hall and stood in the sunlight, kissing, as the blackness slowly took over.

Chapter Three

The Monday following the vow renewal, Kipling stopped by a locally owned coffee shop on his way to the Benedict Industries office near the waterfront. He wasn't a regular patron, but he'd left the house without his normal cup, and since he had to walk past the shop to get to where he was going, he decided to swing by.

He opened the door, not surprised to find the place nearly filled to capacity. What did surprise him was the woman patiently waiting to place her order at the end of the line.

Officer Alyssa Adams.

He still remembered how she felt in his arms while they danced, her body soft and responsive to his. The way her hips swayed against his for those brief precious moments she'd let her guard down.

He couldn't forget how she'd turned him down when he'd asked her to dinner, or how much that refusal had bothered him. But it was more than a case of wounded pride. Wounded pride wouldn't explain why all his fantasies since the day she walked through the doors of Benedict House involved her and her alone. It couldn't explain why no other woman seemed remotely interesting. Nor could it explain why he craved to get in another verbal battle of wits with her. Coming from anyone else, it would be annoying, but from her, it was damn hot.

He walked up behind her and whispered in her ear, "If it isn't Cinderella. Are you supposed to be out this time of day? Aren't you afraid you'll turn into a pumpkin?"

She turned around, but it wasn't her normal *"I can do better than that"* gaze on her face. She looked pale and vulnerable. It took everything in him not to take her in his arms and beg her to tell him what was wrong so he could fix it.

"Alyssa?" he chose to ask instead. "Are you okay?"

Surely it couldn't have been his teasing. She'd never seemed bothered by it before.

"Yes, I'm fine," she said, waving her hand, even though it was obvious she was not.

"Ma'am?" the barista asked.

Alyssa turned away to order her drink. On a whim, he stepped up beside her. "I'll have the same thing."

Alyssa reached for her purse, but Kipling cut her off by handing the cashier his credit card. "Put them both on here."

"You don't—" Alyssa started, but Kipling shook his head.

"Stop," he said, using the tone of voice that people always obeyed. He didn't want to spend what time they had arguing. Still, he was shocked when she didn't say anything further. Her lips were pressed tightly together, and her expression told him where he could shove his credit card, but he'd take that over the look she'd had when she first turned around. "Come and have a seat with me. You're obviously upset about something."

She cocked an eyebrow at him. "And you think you can help?"

"Maybe not, but I'm a good listener."

Much to his surprise, she didn't argue but followed him to a table in the back. He pulled her chair out, not missing the brief look of shock she tried to hide.

"Thank you," she said, and took a sip of her coffee.

When he'd taken his seat across from her, he spoke softly. "Tell me what's going on."

She stared into her coffee so long, he didn't think she would, but then she sighed. "It's the anniversary of my sister's death."

Her confession knocked the wind out of him. He hadn't expected that. "I hate to hear that." He shook his head, unable to even imagine losing a sibling. "How long?"

"I was fifteen."

His chest ached for her. "Losing a sibling is unfathomable to me. It must have been extremely hard as a teenager."

"Yes." She looked up and met his eyes. "Especially since she was murdered."

Alyssa watched his expression contort as understanding dawned.

"My God, Alyssa," he said, horror still on his face. "That's horrible."

He hadn't said the "I'm sorry" line everyone else used when they heard the news. She'd never understood why people felt the need to apologize. It wasn't as if they'd done anything to cause her death.

"It was a long time ago, and I was little when it happened."

"Maybe so," he said. "But it's still impacting you."

She couldn't deny that. "Yes, but it's so much more. It's this case, the missing women, the murdered women. All of it. It's all starting to get to me like never before. I see my sister in every woman in this case, and I can't help but feel as if I've let them all down. I know it's not rational, but that's how I feel. I became a cop to help, and I'm not doing a very good job." She sighed. "I'm tired. Can I say that? I'm tired."

He smiled tentatively, and though she'd always thought of him as attractive, with that easy smile he wore now... trouble and heartache. And she'd had plenty of both. Enough to last for three lifetimes.

"Of course you can admit to being tired. You're only human." He crossed his heart. "Though I promise to keep that last part to myself. I won't tell anyone you're actually a mere mortal."

She allowed herself a small smile. Somehow his teasing made her feel a little better. "Thanks, I appreciate that."

"Tell me about your sister," he said, and though it wasn't a topic she discussed very often or with many people, she felt herself opening up to him.

"She was ten years older than me. I was an 'oops' baby." She'd always known her parents had only wanted one child. And really, it didn't take much thinking to figure it out. A pair of forty-somethings with an almost-teenager and a newborn? "When I was little, Allison looked after me, sometimes more than Mom did, mostly because Mom was too busy with her new husband.

Allison was beautiful and funny, and I wanted to be just like her."

"How so?" he asked.

She smiled, remembering. "I would hang out in her room while she got ready to go out on a date. Like I said, she was beautiful, and I can't remember a weekend when she didn't go out. I was mesmerized watching her put on makeup. All the brushes and bottles. Mom would never let me wear makeup, even for fun. Though I'm pretty certain that was my stepfather's hangup. Anyway, right before she'd finish with her makeup, she'd lean back and say something wasn't right, and then she'd put some lipgloss on me and declare everything was perfect. She made me feel special."

"She sounds like a wonderful sister."

"She was, and everything was prefect until she graduated."

"What happened then?"

"When she was eighteen, shortly after her high school graduation, she came home saying she'd met a man. Not a boy. A man. I thought she made him up because she never brought him to meet us like she'd done with the other guys she went out with. Mom and Dad didn't talk about it much, not around me, anyway, but I could tell they weren't happy with the situation."

While she talked, Kipling listened to every word. She'd always pictured him as the lackadaisical type, and whenever she'd spoken to him in the past, every other word out of his mouth had been sarcastic. To have him ask questions and listen with such intensity made her want to open up and tell him things she'd never told anyone.

"Then she went away. I asked Mom and Dad where she was, but Dad wouldn't say, and Mom just cried. The only thing Mom ever said was that Allison was one of those people who had to learn things the hard way. She never explained what she meant."

Across the table, Kipling still listened, but she bet he was wondering what any of that had to do with her sister being murdered.

"She came back five years later. I remember that better because I was fifteen. Dad told me to wait in my room, and I was so upset he wouldn't even let me see her. To this day, I don't know what happened, but I know there was a lot of yelling, at least from Dad, anyway. Then the front door slammed."

Alyssa remembered running to the upstairs window overlooking the front of the house. All she saw was Allison's back as she ran down the street. Alyssa felt a tear run down her cheek, remembering how her sister never once looked back.

"I went downstairs, but before I could say anything, Dad stopped me and said her name wasn't to be spoken in our house anymore. Mom never stood up to him like I thought she should. She just went along with whatever he said. Less than a week later, Allison was dead. Her body was found in a shelter. Her throat cut. There's never been an arrest."

"Jesus, Alyssa." His face had lost all color. "You mean they never found who did it or why?"

"No, but"—she gave him a weak smile—"it all works out the way it's supposed to, right?"

"It's hard for me to see how that's the case here."

"My sister is the reason I became a cop. I joined the force after college. After her death, I became obsessed with getting criminals off the streets."

"I think that's very admirable," he said softly.

Her face heated as she met his eyes and saw the

sincerity in them. "It's not that big of a deal."

"We'll have to agree to disagree," he said. Before she had a chance to reply, he asked, "Have you looked into your sister's case?"

"Once or twice. Just to see if anything new's turned up. It never has." She bit the corner of her lip.

"There's more you aren't telling me."

It shouldn't have been a surprise he knew she'd held something back. After all, he was a successful businessman, so it stood to reason he could read people easily.

But it did surprise her, and though she hadn't planned to tell him, the whole truth spilled out. "They brought her things by later. I remember being glad they did it during the day so Dad wouldn't know. Mom put it all in the attic, and one day, when I was alone, I looked through it all. There was an envelope in her stuff. Whatever was inside was never found. I don't know if someone took it or if she threw it away somewhere." She took a deep breath. It was too late to stop now. Besides, it was time she told someone. "The envelope was addressed to her, but with no date. For the return, all it said was 'Finition Noire.'"

She paused, waiting for him to make the connection. It didn't take long.

"Finition Noire," he said out loud, as if testing the words. As soon as they left his lips, his eyes grew wide. "That's the name of the fake company that was on the spreadsheets Knox and Bea found and gave to you."

"Yes." She knew those spreadsheets well. The Benedict family had been looking through boxes of papers recently discovered at their house. They'd hoped the boxes contained the information needed to clear Tilly's father's name.

So far they hadn't found anything pertaining to him, but

Alyssa and her team had discovered evidence making them relook at the plane crash, initially considered accidental, that killed both of Kipling's parents. As a result, their cause of death had been changed to murder. Though it was unclear who had orchestrated the crash, it was suspected Finition Noire had some involvement.

His eyes narrowed. "So why is that name in both your sister's case and ours?"

"I don't know. I'm looking into it."

"Do you think that's wise?"

She lifted an eyebrow. "As opposed to not looking into it?"

"Don't play me for a fool."

"That's not what I'm doing," she couldn't help but say.

"I'm serious, Alyssa." That he didn't come back with a snappy comment told her more than if he'd elaborated.

"What?" she asked.

"I agree someone needs to look into this, but I question if you're the right person." He spoke the words softly as if, by doing so, he would be able to lessen the blow. He failed miserably, but she wasn't going to tell him.

"Why would I not be the right person?"

He didn't answer for several long seconds but stared at her with those intense eyes of his. When he finally did speak, his voice was low. "Don't be obtuse, you're too smart to pull it off. You're too emotionally involved in your sister's case. You should hand everything over to someone else."

She knew that, of course, or at least her mind did. Convincing her heart, however, was a different thing altogether. How could anyone else want her sister's case solved more than she did? And how would anyone else possibly work harder to get to the bottom of Finition Noire?

"It's not happening," she told him.

"Does your supervisor know about the connection?"

Hell no. She wasn't stupid. If he knew, he would take her off the case, no questions asked. But she'd be damned if she'd admit that to Kipling. "I don't see how you have any right to know the particulars of an ongoing investigation."

Kipling gave a curt nod as if that was the response he'd expected. "I'll take that as a no."

"I really don't care what you take it as. It's the truth." She wouldn't put it past Kipling to call her supervisor and tell him, but she wasn't going to beg him not to, either. "I know how it looks."

He leaned forward, and she found herself doing the same. He appeared altogether like the no-nonsense businessman he was, and she felt sorry for those who found themselves opposite him in the boardroom. Even more so, she hated herself for being attracted to him. Seriously, here she was, sitting across from a man who had the potential to ruin her career, and all she could think about was how good his arms had felt around her when they danced?

"I don't think you do know how it looks," he said. "You're the one talking about how tired you are, how the cases are getting to you like never before, and how you feel guilty. I'm worried about you, emotionally. It's not healthy to live in the past."

There was little else he could have said that would have shocked her more. "I'm fine."

"No, you're not, and before you decide to argue with me, I'm just calling it the way I see it."

She resisted the temptation to flip him off and say, *"See this,"* but it was hard. "No," she said, instead. "You're calling it like you *think* you see it. You forget that *you're* emotionally involved in the case too."

A look of satisfaction covered his face. "So you admit

you're emotionally involved."

"My sister was murdered. I think that automatically qualifies for emotional involvement."

"My point exactly."

She didn't know how to respond. He had her mind going in so many different directions, she wasn't sure how to continue. She finally settled by saying, "You would do the same thing. Can you honestly tell me that you'd step aside if one of your brothers was murdered?"

"That's a moot point because, one, we're not talking about me and, two, I'm not a police officer."

She hated he was right. For weeks she'd been debating telling her boss everything and stepping down from the case. But every time she had a chance, she couldn't. She was Allison's sister, for crying out loud; how could she give up? Maybe it was fate she wound up on the Benedict case, because if she hadn't, a connection between the two cases would have never been made. She'd be damned if Kipling Benedict was going to step in *now* and mess everything up.

"We're finished here." She pushed back from the table. "Thank you very much for your offer to sit down. I'm so glad I accepted because I feel much better now," she said, her voice dripping with sarcasm.

Kipling lifted his coffee cup in a mock salute. "Anytime you need someone to ride your ass, I'm your man."

A sudden image of her on all fours with Kipling behind her popped into her head, freezing her in place. *Oh, dear sweet Lord.*

"You have a horrible poker face." Kipling grinned. "But I'm your man for that too."

"You are..." she started, but her mind blanked.

"Your every dirty fantasy come to life? The man you dream about when you're in bed alone? An amazing sex god?" He leaned back in his chair, and her eyes couldn't move from his broad shoulders and chest. It was far too easy to picture how he'd look without the suit.

"You wish," she replied, hoping her voice and expression didn't betray her thoughts.

"I've never denied it."

Her heart raced at his calm acknowledgment of the fact he'd fantasized about her. Far too late, she realized she had no snappy comeback. In fact, she had no comeback at all. Without saying a word, she spun on her heel and walked away.

At the last minute, she glanced over her shoulder. "You'll never know what it's like to lose a sister."

* * *

Kipling watched Alyssa's retreat, but not with the mirth he'd portrayed to her. What the ever-loving fuck had gotten into him that he'd flirt with a woman he'd been mad as hell with mere seconds before? What was it about Officer Adams that had him want to beat his head against a wall and rip every stitch of clothing off her body in equal measure?

He'd hoped dancing with her would get her out of his system. Though now that he had time to think, it made no sense that, in holding her for a dance, he'd no longer yearn to hold her. Of course his plan hadn't worked. It'd failed miserably. Instead of being satisfied with the fact that her embrace held nothing, he'd found the opposite to be true. Holding her for one dance only increased his desire to hold her again and again. Preferably naked.

He'd joked about his being her every dirty fantasy when, in fact, she had quickly become his. Even his subconscious agreed. At night he dreamed of a sultry police officer who loved to give in bed just as hard as she gave out of bed, and whose sex drive matched his own.

"Excuse me, sir," a waitress interrupted. "Can I get some of this out of your way?"

He nodded and checked his phone for messages. Nothing that couldn't wait for his return to the office. He remained at the table for a few more minutes, taking the final sips of his coffee before leaving.

From there, it was a short walk to the harborside offices of Benedict Industries. Keaton and Tilly were working off-site today and Knox and Bea were away on their second honeymoon. Kipling looked forward to a relatively quiet and uneventful day.

He needed a slow day so he could think about what to do with Alyssa. How to move forward with her. To not only get to know her better, but to continue to connect with her on an emotional level like earlier this morning. He unlocked the door and stepped inside with a chuckle. He knew exactly what he wanted to do with Alyssa. After their coffee chat, unfortunately, the odds of that ever happening were somewhere between slim and none, leaning heavily toward the none.

He was surprised she'd opened up about her sister. Alyssa didn't come across as one who shared that type of information lightly. It probably only happened because the day itself made her emotional.

He tried to imagine losing one of his brothers in such a violent way, but he couldn't. The very thought made his chest hurt. Alyssa had been so much younger when she lost her sister. He had a new respect and appreciation for her, though neither one voided the fact that she shouldn't be on the case.

Sitting at his desk, he sighed, unsure of what, if anything, he should say or do about the case. He wanted to trust her when she said it wouldn't impact her adversely, but how could he be certain? From everything he saw, Alyssa was whip smart and not the type to let emotions get in her way. But having a family member murdered, that case going unsolved for years and years, and it dictating what she did for a living...

He drummed his fingers on the top of his desk. He just didn't know.

His desk phone rang, and he welcomed the opportunity to think and talk about something else.

"Kipling Benedict," he answered.

"Mr. Benedict," the person on the other end of the phone said in a voice so low, Kipling had to strain his ears to hear. "I know you're a very busy man, so I'll keep this short and to the point. I have your sister. She's alive for now. If you want to keep her that way, you'll follow the instructions I'll be sending your way soon."

Before Kipling could reply, the line went dead. He stared at the handset for several long minutes, his heart pounding madly. He forced himself to think rationally. No one could have possibly kidnapped Jade. Hadn't Keaton sworn up and down that she was half ninja? Sure, she had been thin and run-down-looking the last time he saw her, but she was smart.

He tapped his pen on his desk, trying to think of what else could explain the call. In his head, he heard Alyssa snap at him that he'd never know what it was like to lose a sister. *Alyssa.* He snorted and dialed the phone number he'd memorized but never used.

"Officer Adams," Alyssa answered just as quickly and efficiently as he'd suspected she would.

"Well played, Adams." He relaxed, leaning back in his chair. "You almost had me for a minute."

"I would say *thank you*, Benedict, but I have no idea what you're talking about."

"I find lying to be a most unattractive quality in a woman."

"I know you find this hard to believe, but I'm not trying to attract you. Even if I was, I still don't know what you're talking about."

Right. Like he believed either of those statements to be true. Of course, he really hadn't expected her to admit to setting up the phone call. At least, not right away. He could wait. "If that's the way you want to play it for now, I'll go along with you. But be sure to tell whoever you got to make the phone call that he has the sinister villain voice nailed. I actually thought he had my sister for a minute."

"Kipling," she said, sounding a bit worried. "What are you talking about? You don't have a sister."

He realized his oversight as soon as the words left his mouth. He felt clammy, sick, and couldn't speak as the truth hit him. Alyssa didn't know. No one except his brothers, Tilly, and Bea knew.

The half sister he and his brothers had only recently found out about. Kaja, or Jade, as she preferred to be called. Kipling had only met her once, and he hadn't been overly kind to her. But to be fair, at the time he hadn't known they were related and he'd thought she'd been breaking into his house.

"Kipling?" Alyssa asked again.

He cleared his throat and managed to find his voice. "Officer Adams, would it be possible for you to come by the office near the harbor? I need to report a kidnapping."

Chapter Four

Alyssa hurried to her unmarked car, her mind working overtime trying to understand Kipling's phone call. Nothing within the past five minutes had made any sense. The only thing she was certain of was the fear Kipling couldn't hide in his voice.

She nearly ran to her car after the call ended. She wasn't sure he realized exactly how he sounded, but it shook her to her core. Even now, minutes after the call, her hands trembled.

On the way to his office, she went over in her head what she knew. Kipling had received a phone call from someone with a sinister voice. That person had mentioned a sister and a kidnapping. For some reason the combination of the two hit a nerve with him and he'd asked her to stop by. She'd worked numerous kidnapping cases in her career, but never before had she experienced the feeling of foreboding she did at that moment. It reminded her of the feeling she'd had right before learning her sister was dead.

And that scared the hell out of her.

She pulled into a public parking lot near the building

housing the harbor offices of Benedict Industries. Hopefully Kipling would make more sense in person than he had on the phone.

She stepped into the office to find him pacing in the front room. He turned toward her, and his harrowing expression froze her in her tracks.

"Kipling?" she asked.

"Thanks for coming so quickly."

"Tell me what's going on."

His brief hesitation surprised her—at least, until she realized that whatever he had to tell her was going to cost him something. He waved her toward his office.

"Let's go sit down," he said. "I'm not expecting anyone, but given recent circumstances, I'd prefer we be as private as possible."

She followed him to the large office in the back and sat down on the small love seat he had in a sitting area off to the side. He followed, taking a seat in the armchair across from her, and dropped his head into his hands. He took a deep breath and looked up.

"God," he said. "Where to start?"

She couldn't help him, so she remained silent and waited for him to continue.

"We've recently discovered our father wasn't...damn." He grimaced. "He cheated on our mom."

Alyssa would have liked to have said she was surprised, but the truth was, she'd seen too much to be shocked about a wealthy man—hell, any man—cheating on his wife.

"Not only that," Kipling said. "He fathered a child. A daughter. We don't know who the woman is he had an affair with, but we suspect she's dead." He closed his eyes. "The daughter is Jade."

Her mouth fell open in shock. "Jade? You mean *Jade*,

32

Jade?" Her head told her it had to be someone else. Surely it couldn't be the woman Alyssa had assumed was a criminal trying to break into Benedict House, only to discover the woman had been Bea's client as well as the person who'd helped Keaton rescue Tilly by showing him a secret passage he hadn't know existed in his own house. The youngest Benedict brother had mentioned being impressed by the numerous knives strapped to the woman's body.

Kipling gave a smile that wasn't really a smile. "Yes, the little ninja. And to answer your next question, no, we didn't know she was our sister when she spent that night at the house."

Jade is their sister? Her mind kept repeating the question. It didn't seem possible. Tilly claimed to have seen Jade before, in a homeless shelter, but according to Tilly, Jade might have had a hand in the disappearance of one of the residents. She shook her head. *No way.*

"We were just as shocked as you look," he said.

"You have a sister," she said.

"A half sister, but yes."

Suddenly, she remembered why she was sitting across from him in the first place. "Someone's kidnapped her."

"It appears that way."

But there was more to it, and her mind worked frantically trying to sort everything out. "Whoever has her knows who she is. Or maybe she found out somehow."

"I thought about both of those," Kipling said, "but I'm not sure how likely it is because only a handful of people know the truth. That I'm aware of, anyway."

She leaned forward so she could ensure she had his undivided attention. "You might be able to disregard the unlikely in your business, Mr. Benedict, but when it comes to what I do, ignoring the unlikely is liable to lead you into trouble. Also, don't forget the last time any of us saw her was at your house, and a good number of those present, yourself included, made no secret of the fact that they thought she was a criminal."

He didn't say anything. He just looked at her in his studious way that made her feel like an anomaly.

"What?" she finally asked.

He grinned, and it appeared that he'd almost returned to normal. At least on the outside, anyway. His color wasn't nearly as pale, and he no longer looked scared to death. "Sitting here, talking to you, listening to the way you reason and argue with me, on top of knowing what a good police officer you are?" He shook his head. "I actually have hope that we'll find her."

She cocked an eyebrow. "I'm obviously missing something here because I don't have a clue as to what you're talking about."

He stood, and she didn't like the feeling of him looming over her, so she also stood.

"I'd like to offer you a proposition," he said.

Hell, could he not be serious for longer than five seconds? "Oh, really?"

"Look at your mind going straight to the gutter." He made a tsking noise. "It's not that type of proposition. Though if you'd like to discuss *that* kind later...?"

"No." She crossed her arms across her chest because, no matter how infuriating she thought him, his close proximity paired with the images of "*that* kind" had her body craving things it had no business craving. "Explain your proposition."

He assessed her once more, perhaps to see if she was serious. She leveled her gaze at him to prove she was.

He nodded. "Here's my offer. I won't tell your supervisor about your personal connection with the case, and in exchange, you will allow me to work with you. No secrets. You know something, you tell me."

Besides his keeping quiet about her connection, it sounded like a horrible deal. He would get complete access to the case, but other than his silence, what did he bring to the table?

"I know you're a powerful businessman and incredibly successful, but let's face it." She waved her hand around the room. "You're a shipping expert. How are you going to advance the case? I'm sure I don't have to remind you that every family member of every missing person wants them found, yet we don't invite them to work with us."

"Surely you aren't that naive."

She tried to take a step backward but hit the love seat. He towered over her. She felt the heat radiate from his body, and couldn't stop wondering how his body would feel against hers. Naked. Or above hers. Also naked…

He chuckled. "Someone's thinking naughty thoughts again, aren't they?" he asked in a low, seductive voice that sent shivers up her spine. "Whatever am I going to do with you?"

She had a top ten list ready in response to his question, but she pushed all thoughts of it aside. "How about we start with you answering the question?" she asked, pleased her voice didn't tremble.

"Okay," he said. "But I thought that much was obvious. Yes, I'm a shipping expert, but remember, that has made me wealthy. Very wealthy. Obscenely wealthy. Which means I can fund your investigation into Finition Noire and give you more resources than the Charleston PD could ever dream of being able to afford."

She was crazy to even think about it…wasn't she?

She told herself she wasn't going to risk her career for money. Especially *his* money. She'd arrested him once, for crying out loud.

But the more she thought about it, the more she liked the idea.

She would have to quit the force. Not that quitting made what she was thinking about doing right. But with the availability of funds, she would be able to do more on the case. And hadn't she been thinking about leaving the force anyway?

God, she was so tempted.

"You're thinking about it, aren't you?" he asked.

"You know I am."

"Do it, Alyssa," he said in the same seductive voice he'd used previously. "You know we'll be good together."

Why did she get the feeling he wasn't talking about the cases?

"Would we?" she challenged him. "I have a feeling we'd spend most of the time arguing and getting on each other's nerves."

He laughed softly. "Of course we would. That's what's going to make this so interesting."

"I need to think about it first," she said. Preferably somewhere he wasn't. She didn't want to allow him the opportunity to influence her decision. Or at least that's what she told herself. The truth was, she knew she'd more than likely already made up her mind, but she didn't want him to know.

"Offer stands until tomorrow at noon," he said.

She raised an eyebrow. "That's not very much time."

"You've already decided and you know it. You want to make me sweat." His cocky grin was back. "Something you should know about me before you agree to this is that I very rarely sweat about anything."

"You're an ass." She pushed him aside and walked to the door of his office. She turned around before walking out. "It may not be over this, but I guarantee I'll make you sweat about something."

"I'm counting on it," he said, wearing a look that somehow managed to be playful while still carrying a hint of wicked intent.

Chapter Five

Kipling left his office shortly after Alyssa did. He knew he wouldn't be able to concentrate on anything following the phone call and the subsequent conversation with Alyssa. He walked slowly back to the house.

Without Alyssa nearby to tease, his thoughts went back to Jade.

He remembered the day Knox found the birth certificate in the oven of the house he'd bought to renovate with Bea. He'd thought Knox was playing a joke on him at first. Jade was their sister? The young woman half the family thought was out to get them, and the other half saw as a misunderstood street-rat ninja? It didn't seem possible.

But then he'd looked at the birth certificate, and it seemed real enough. Knox had gone a step further and called the Division of Vital Records to verify its legitimacy. He'd hung up the phone, looking pale, and said simply, "It's legit."

With those two little words, it was as if Kipling had been punched in the stomach. He had a sister, a little sister, and he'd all but thrown her out of the house. Looking back at that day now, it was obvious she needed help and he'd done nothing, *nothing* to help.

He cringed every time he thought about that night. He tried to tell himself that, based on the information he'd had, his actions were justifiable. But justification didn't make him feel better, because he knew he'd acted like a horse's ass to her.

It came as a surprise to no one other than Bea when Jade slipped out of the house in the middle of the night, leaving through the secret passage that was so secret, neither he nor his brothers had known of its existence until she'd told Keaton. Since that night, no one had heard from her. Knox had gone online and exhausted his extensive search capabilities, but every lead he chased turned out to be a dead end. They'd wanted to find her guardian, if nothing else, but again, nothing.

Kipling couldn't help but think the guardian was related to her current situation. It seemed odd they couldn't find any information on the man or woman.

He ran a hand through his hair. He hated to do it, but he had to call Knox and have him and Bea come home early. Maybe, with Alyssa's help, they could find something new and finally get to the bottom of this. Jade was in danger, and they had to rescue her.

He arrived home to find Tilly and Keaton working in the home office. He must've looked bad, as they both looked up and suddenly wore concerned expressions.

"What?" Kipling asked.

"You look horrible," Keaton said. "What happened?"

So much for his little flirtation with Alyssa helping him look better. He sighed. "I got a call at the office. They said Jade has been kidnapped. If I want to see her alive again, I'll follow all the instructions they'll be sending." He hadn't planned on spitting it out like that, but there it was.

"Shit, are you serious?" Keaton asked.

"I called Knox, and he and Bea are coming home early." Kipling hated they had to cut their honeymoon short, but there was no other choice. "I'm going to have him relook at a few things. And you two should know I've asked Alyssa Adams to help us."

"Isn't that her job?" Keaton asked.

"I asked her to join us in an unofficial capacity." Kipling was prepared to field more questions, but instead, only a look passed between Keaton and Tilly. "I have no way of knowing if she'll agree or not," he added, and they both turned their attention back to him.

"She won't." Tilly shook her head. "She'll think that would be unethical."

Though he hated to do so, Kipling had to admit she was probably right.

"I can't believe you asked her in the first place," Tilly said.

Keaton gave her a funny look. "Really? I can."

Thankfully, the doorbell rang, and Kipling was spared further funny glances from the couple. He met their long-time housekeeper, Maggie, in the hallway and told her he'd get the door. He opened it to find Alyssa on the other side.

He couldn't stop a huge grin from appearing at the sight of her. "I must say, Officer Adams, I didn't expect you to decide that quickly."

"If I remember correctly, you told me I'd already decided." She shrugged. "Since you told me I couldn't make you sweat, I figured why expend the energy?"

He leaned in as if to tell her a secret. "I never said you couldn't make me sweat. I said I very rarely sweat over anything. I can think of several things we could do that would lead to sweating on my part."

"A condition of my working with you is that you have to stop with the not-so-subtle sexual innuendos. As much fun as it is to spar with you, we need to keep this professional."

Damn, he liked her. "It's August in Charleston, Alyssa. All I have to do is walk outside to sweat. You're the one making everything sexual."

"If you let her come inside so you could close the door, no one would have to sweat," Keaton said from the hallway.

"Now I know which Benedict brother got the brains." Alyssa swept her way inside, past Kipling, like he wasn't even there. "Hello, Keaton. Tilly."

They both said hello to her and then Tilly led them all into the kitchen, where she'd made a cake earlier in the day.

"I planned on having it after dinner," she said, slicing everyone a piece. "But I think we all need some now."

"I agree," Keaton said. "Cut me a bigger piece than that."

"I'll take a small one, thanks," Alyssa said.

They all took their cake and sat around the kitchen table. Kipling waited for Alyssa to sit down and then took the seat beside her. Not that she noticed—she was too wrapped up in Tilly's cake.

"This is divine," Alyssa said, digging into her slice.

"You should have gotten a bigger slice." Keaton held up his overflowing plate.

Alyssa laughed. "I really should have."

Kipling realized it was the first time he'd heard her laugh, and he felt strangely jealous it wasn't the result of something he'd said.

Across the table, Keaton had finished his monstrous

slice and was watching Alyssa carefully. "So," the youngest brother said. "You're going to work with us?"

Alyssa wiped her mouth. "Yes, I came over to tell your brother I'm going to resign from the police department. I'm not going to tell them why."

Another one of those looks passed between Keaton and Tilly. Kipling did his best not to roll his eyes.

"Decided to come over to the dark side?" Keaton teased.

"Something like that." Alyssa finished her cake and put down her fork. "I was wondering as I drove over here, when did you find out about Jade?"

"Someone put her birth certificate in the house Knox and Bea are renovating," Keaton said. "They found it not long after he was released from the hospital."

"But before that, I found a birth certificate hidden in some old files." Kipling looked at Alyssa. "It had the child listed as Jane Doe, so we didn't know it was Jade at that point."

"We also thought she was dead," Keaton added.

"That's strange," Alyssa said. "Why would you think that?"

"We thought we had her death certificate," Keaton said. "But Bea was able to determine it was a fake."

"And," Kipling added, "she found the date of the fake death certificate was very close to the time Tilly's father was fired for supposed espionage."

Keaton placed his hand over Tilly's. "But we think Tilly's dad was set up. It never seemed like something he'd do, and we've been looking over all the old records to try and prove it."

Something struck Kipling at that moment, and he couldn't believe he'd never put the two together before.

"Knox told me once that Bea was looking into similar records when she was attacked the first time."

Alyssa whipped a notebook out of her purse. "Wait a minute," she said. "I have to write this down. I want make sure I don't forget anything."

Kipling watched as she wrote and didn't miss her frown. "What?" he asked.

"I've got: Tilly's dad, Jade, your parents' deaths, and the attacks and threats on Bea. Bea was attacked shortly after she started looking into Tilly's dad, and he was fired around the date on the death certificate." The frown hadn't left her face. "I'm missing something. I know I am."

"We all are," Kipling agreed.

"What do you know about Jade's mother?" Alyssa asked.

Kipling shook his head. "Nothing."

"Who was Jade's guardian?" Alyssa asked.

"That's another thing we don't know," Kipling said. "Knox has been trying to find out but, so far, hasn't had any luck."

"He's a hacker. During the summers while he was in college, he did some work in the Middle East for the US government," Keaton added, and Kipling shot him a dirty look. "Sorry, man, but if she's going to be working with us, she should know."

"Part of the problem," Kipling picked up, hoping Alyssa would ignore the hacking part, at least for now, "is we aren't sure we have her real name. She gave us Kaja Jade Mann, but there doesn't seem to be a record of such a person."

Alyssa didn't react in any way other than to tap her pen against the pad of paper. Normally, such a habit would have annoyed Kipling, but for some reason, she made it hot. Of course, it seemed like he felt that way about everything she did.

The tapping stopped abruptly. "I know." Alyssa reached into her purse and pulled something out. "Where did Jade sleep, and which bathroom did she use when she was here?"

Kipling raised an eyebrow.

She sighed. "I'm looking for hair."

"You won't find it on the sheets she used, and Maggie will take it as an insult if you suggest as much."

"Let me see the bathroom she used, then. Maybe there's some hair left in a brush or something."

Kipling nodded. "Come with me. I'll take you."

He led her down the hall into the room Jade had used the one time she stayed at Benedict House. There was also a connecting bathroom. Maggie would have changed the sheets, but there was a possibility Jade used the brush in the bathroom if she didn't have one.

Alyssa went straight for the drawers in the bathroom and smiled when she found the hairbrush. "There's hair in it. Has anyone else used this brush?"

Kipling shook his head. "The last person to stay in that room before Jade was a distant cousin from England, months ago. I don't think the brush was in the bathroom then, and Maggie restocked the bathroom after he left."

Alyssa collected several strands of hair and placed them in what Kipling now saw was an evidence envelope.

"What exactly are you doing?" he asked.

"I'm going to submit this hair to the lab," Alyssa said.

"For DNA?" Kipling had to admit it was a good idea and one he hadn't thought of before.

"Mitochondrial DNA," she clarified.

"What's the difference?"

"Mitochondrial DNA is what we sometimes use in kidnapping cases. However, it's not the entire genotype, and it's not unique. It's passed down through the maternal line, so for example, my mitochondrial DNA is exactly like my sister's and my mother's."

"How will this help find Jade?"

"For one, if any maternal family member of hers is in the database, we'll find them, and that might help us find her."

That was good enough in his book. "How long will it take to get results?"

She had that glimmer of excitement in her eyes. The one he loved so much. "Don't worry about it. I know people."

Chapter Six

The day after agreeing to work with Kipling and turning in her resignation, Alyssa stood in her bedroom, brushing out her hair. Because she wore it in a ponytail all day, she loved nothing more than taking it down. In fact, it was one of her favorite parts of her day. She flipped her head over and brushed through the tangles until the strands were smooth and crackled. Once she put the brush down, she scratched her scalp. It felt so good, she almost groaned.

She still couldn't believe she'd told Kipling all that information about Allison. Likewise, why had it been so easy to tell him anything concerning her sister? Sure, it had felt good to talk about everything, but hell, she'd never told *anyone* about Allison.

That wasn't the only thing bothering her. Kipling was on that list too. Why was it impossible to get the man out of her hair? And did she even want to?

Stupid question. No. She didn't want Kipling *out* of her hair. The exact opposite, in fact—she wanted him *in* her hair.

47

With her head still flipped over, she ran her fingers through her hair again, pretending they were his. Would he be gentle or rough? In her fantasy he would be both. He'd start gentle, and the more aroused he became, the rougher he'd get. And because it was her fantasy, the closer he got to his release, the tighter he'd fist her hair. She buried her fingers in her hair and pulled. That wasn't enough, so she grabbed two tight fistfuls and gave them a good, solid yank. Then she let go with a sigh.

It was nowhere close to being as good when she did it herself. How long had it been since she'd had rough, hair-pulling sex? Definitely before her last relationship.

As always, her stomach churned at the thought of her ex, Mac. And like every time before, she couldn't stop the almost unbearable feelings of guilt and shame over the realization she'd been in a long-term relationship with a man who turned out to be a wanted murder. It seemed unlikely she'd ever completely get over the relationship.

With a sigh, she brushed her hair all over, one last time, and put the hairbrush down.

Earlier, she'd lain out the outfit she planned to wear, but now she debated if she wanted to jog. She snorted. She never *wanted* to jog, but it was necessary in order for her to stay in shape.

With that, she pulled out a sports bra and placed it on the bed, when she heard a floorboard creak from the front part of her house.

She froze.

It wasn't unheard of for her house to creak. After all, all houses did. But she knew the noises her house made, and that wasn't one of them.

Her heart pounded. She strained her ears, trying to listen for anything that sounded out of the ordinary. But all she heard was her own heartbeat and her breathing. She held completely still, although she wasn't sure why. If anyone was in the house, they knew she was as well.

She remained in place for several long minutes, trying to be completely still and closing her eyes to pick up on anything unusual. Before moving, she looked across the room at her weapon. It was too far away to reach from her current location, and because she knew her house so well, she knew there was no way to get to it without walking across the squeaky floorboards in her bedroom.

There.

Was that another squeak? The silence in her room was so complete it echoed loudly in her head. She kept thinking she heard things but couldn't tell if they were real or not.

Damn it all. If someone was in her house, she wanted to be armed before meeting them. She stepped toward the gun, determined to get it before running into the intruder. She eased her foot onto the squeaky floorboard and gently pressed down on it.

Right as the floor moaned a faint creak underneath her foot, she heard the clicking of the front door. She froze in place. Had someone entered or had they left?

Unwilling to wait any longer, she ran across the room, grabbed her gun, and headed toward the front of the house. Through the window, she watched a nondescript black car pull out of her driveway. Of course, there was no license plate on the car.

She took a deep breath. More than likely, whoever was in the house had left, but she wouldn't be able to rest until she knew for certain. Gun in hand, she searched every room.

Nothing was out of place until she reached the kitchen.

There, in the middle of her table and placed where she couldn't miss it, was a perfect black rose.

* * *

"Mr. Kipling?" Maggie asked from the doorway of his office.

Kipling looked up from the contract he'd been reading and pushed back from his desk. "Did I miss dinner again? I'm so sorry. I seriously don't know how you put up my worthless self."

"No, sir. Dinner still has a while to cook." Maggie gave him a big grin. "It's Ms. Adams. She's back."

"Officer Adams?" He looked behind her to see if she had followed Maggie.

"I told her to wait in the foyer. I wasn't sure where you wanted to talk with her."

Kipling narrowed his eyes at the much-too-helpful Maggie.

As expected, she continued, "I thought you might like to invite her to dinner. I cooked plenty, and from the looks of it, she could use some home cooking."

"I'll ask her if she's interested." He walked swiftly to the foyer. It wasn't like Alyssa to come by this time of the evening, and he feared something had happened.

She stood facing away from him, and when she turned around, his chest constricted. Not only because of the look in her eyes, but because of what she held. A black rose.

"Kipling," she said. "I'm sorry. I didn't mean to ruin your evening."

He held a hand up. "Don't apologize. Ever. You are welcome to come here whenever you need to." He nodded toward the rose. "Where did you get that?"

"It was left in my house."

"Inside your house?"

"Yes, I was upstairs and thought I heard something downstairs. I crossed the room to get my gun, but whoever it was ran outside before I could get to them. This was sitting on the kitchen table."

He took a deep breath to calm down because, if he didn't, he'd blow a gasket. "Come in here and sit down," he said when he could talk without clenching his teeth, and he led her to the living room. She sat in an armchair, and he took a seat on the ottoman in front of her. "Someone was in your house at the same time you were?"

She tried to put on a brave face, but he saw the fear hidden in her eyes. "Yes, but I had a gun."

He leaned forward, resting his hands on his knees. "Alyssa, I don't give a damn if you had a whole arsenal. Someone was in your house. You're in law enforcement. I can't imagine your place is easy to get into. How did they manage?"

"I have no idea." She looked dejected at her admission, and he was well aware of how much it pained her to say those words.

"I'm willing to bet you don't have a spare key under your doormat."

She narrowed her eyes. "Seriously?"

He held his hands up. "I'm thinking of the easiest way to break into your place."

"Think harder."

"Any neighbors or friends with a key?"

"Just my friend Janie and..." Her eyes grew big.

"What?" he asked after she didn't say anything.

"Just a thought." She drummed her fingers on the arm

of the chair. "Mac had the keys to my house. After I...after he...died..." She closed her eyes.

Kipling remembered teasing her once about her ex who ended up being a murderer. At the time, he hadn't thought about how it'd affect her. Damn, he was an ass for saying anything about what had to be a painful issue for her.

He reached out his hand. They were close enough he could just brush her knee. A light touch to let her know he was with her. Not that he understood, because there was no way he could, but a silent show of support. At least, that's how he hoped it came across. Maybe it worked; she didn't jerk away.

No, if anything, her body seemed to relax. Possibly, he only saw what he wanted, but it truly appeared as if his touch calmed her. An urge to gather her in his arms and protect her filled him unexpectedly.

"Take a deep breath and tell me," he whispered, somehow feeling that this was an important step in their relationship. Outside of the first time they'd met, she'd never mentioned Mac.

Her eyes were open, and she took several deep breaths. "Sorry, it's not easy for me talk about this," she said with a weak smile.

"I imagine not." He squeezed her knee and sat back, giving her space.

"Mac had a key," she said. "I don't know what happened to it. After."

"We have to assume it fell into the wrong hands and whoever has it knows it's a key to your house."

"I'll call tomorrow and have my locks changed." She sighed and ran her fingers through her hair.

Kipling tried not to pay attention to her hair, but it was easier said than done. Especially since she normally wore it up and this was one of the few times he'd seen it down. He told himself to focus on the issue at hand and not how soft he imagined her hair would be or what it would smell like. "If they got in once, they could get in again," he said. "If you would like, you're more than welcome to stay here."

"Thank you, but no," she replied in a clipped voice, her lips pressed into a thin line.

He didn't have a damn clue what he'd done or said to elicit such a response. "Based on your reply, I get the feeling I should apologize for something, but I'm at a loss as to what."

"I'm not Tilly or Bea," she said. "I'm not your girlfriend or your wife, so no, I'm not staying here. I'll get a hotel room tonight, and tomorrow someone will come out and replace my locks. Everything will go back to normal."

"Then I apologize if my offer came across as anything other than one friend reaching out to another." He crossed his arms and leveled his gaze. "I assume it's safe to call us friends, or is that pushing the envelope as well?"

She didn't shrink from his stare. "I'm okay with friends."

"I have to be honest with you. I'm not sure I want to be your friend. What I'd like to be is a bit more intimate than mere friends."

Her cheeks flushed with a hint of color, and she refused to meet his gaze.

Before she had the chance to reply, Keaton and Tilly's voices filled the room. Tilly entered the living room first, though Keaton was right behind her.

Tilly was all smiles as she spoke to her fiancé. "I told you it was Alyssa's car." She turned to Alyssa and at once seemed to be aware that she'd walked in on something. "Should we leave?"

Kipling stood up. "No, of course not. We were just chatting. Nothing important," he said. "Alyssa, come have dinner with us. You'll upset Maggie if you don't stay."

She frowned. "I don't know. I should probably make sure I can get a room somewhere."

"Have dinner with us," Kipling said. "And if I have to call everyone I know in Charleston to ensure you have a place to sleep tonight, I will."

Alyssa didn't look convinced, but she followed him out of the room.

"What was all that about?" Kipling heard Keaton ask Tilly.

"I think your brother lied to us when he said we didn't interrupt anything," Tilly said in a loud whisper.

Chapter Seven

A lyssa saw Bea and Knox were already in the dining room. She'd heard they'd cut their honeymoon short, but she hadn't known for sure when they'd make it back.

Bea looked up from her conversation with Knox as they all entered, but her smile faded at the sight of Alyssa. Knox reacted immediately, sitting up straighter and looking around, trying to find what had scared his wife.

Bea pointed to the rose Alyssa had in her hand. "Where...where did you get that?"

Alyssa didn't miss the *What in the hell?* look Knox shot his oldest brother. Kipling stepped closer to Alyssa and put a hand at the small of her back. She relaxed almost immediately.

"Alyssa found the rose inside her house this evening." Kipling pulled out a chair out for her and ensured she was settled before taking his own seat. "If you remember, it was a rose like this one that led to my unfortunate arrest some months ago."

It was a day Alyssa would never forget. The body of a dancer from a local gentlemen's club had been found, and since several people had seen the dancer talking to Kipling not long before she died, Alyssa and her partner stopped by Benedict House to question him. They were getting nowhere until Alyssa pulled out a black rose. Kipling asked when the police had taken it out of his car, but the rose had been found on the dancer's body. To this day, Alyssa wasn't sure which one of them was more surprised when she arrested him.

Bea still hadn't regained all her color. "There were some of them in an arrangement at my father's service. I remember thinking they were the creepiest flowers I'd ever seen." She shivered. "I still do."

"We always assumed, later," Knox said, continuing to keep a careful eye on the woman at his side, "that it was Tom who had arranged for the flowers and the note."

Alyssa froze. "There was a note?"

"I've been working on these chickens all afternoon," Maggie said, entering the dining room and carrying a tray that looked as if it weighed more than she did. But Alyssa knew from previous visits that Maggie wouldn't accept help from anyone. "And I don't want to hear one more word about roses or anything else unpleasant. Do you understand? It'll mess up your digestion."

As always, no one argued with Maggie.

Bea and Knox had excused themselves from dinner before everyone else finished, but they were waiting in the living room when everyone gathered there afterward.

Bea passed something from her hand to Alyssa. "It's the note from the black roses at my father's service," she said.

It was much too late to attempt to get fingerprints off the note, and Alyssa wasn't sure it would have mattered anyway. "Interesting that this person always uses black roses."

"They aren't black," Kipling said.

"What?" Alyssa held up the flower in question. "It looks black to me."

Kipling shook his head. "It's a very deep crimson. I did a little bit of research when I kept getting them."

"Interesting." Alyssa twirled the rose. "It still looks black to me."

"Just because they look that way doesn't mean they are." Kipling took the rose from her. "Also, these are so rare they're almost extinct. And they only grow in Turkey."

Knox gave a low whistle and slipped his arm around Bea. "That's a rather extravagant threat, wouldn't you say? Why spend so much money?"

"Unless you really want to make a statement," Alyssa said.

"Is there any way Tom could have afforded anything close to what I assume those cost?" Bea asked. "If not, it seems to lend credibility to our idea of someone who is not only the mastermind but also has fairly deep pockets and a staff of minions."

"Once more narrowing the field of potential suspects," Alyssa said.

"I can pull a list of nurseries in Turkey that export those roses," Knox said. "It shouldn't take long at all."

"Thank you. I'll start making phone calls while my locks are changed." Alyssa glanced at her watch. "Speaking of, I need to head out."

"I'll go with you and see that you get settled," Kipling said. "Since you're being stubborn and won't stay here."

"I'll be fine on my own. I don't need you to follow me."

"I know that," Kipling said in a low voice. "I want to go for me, so I can make sure you're safe."

She didn't roll her eyes like she wanted to. Instead, she

told herself he was only looking out for her best interest. Besides, even if she argued, it wouldn't do any good because he would just do whatever he wanted and follow anyway. And though she'd never admit it to him, it was sweet.

"Let's go," she said.

Kipling looked momentarily stunned at her agreement, but he collected himself quickly and walked outside with her. "You know where you're staying?"

She named a middle-of-the-road hotel. It wasn't a roach motel, but she suspected it was nowhere near the opulence of any place he'd typically stay.

"Lead the way," he said.

She waited for him to get in his car, and then she drove to the hotel where she hoped to stay for the night. It wasn't far from Benedict House, and for that, she was glad. If something else were to come up or, god forbid, happen to her, he could arrive quickly.

He didn't get out of his car after pulling into the *Check In Only* spot next to her. Though his windows were tinted, they allowed her to see he was talking on the phone. Her stomach twisted, but she wasn't sure why. She decided not to get out until he did.

Three minutes later, he opened his door and motioned for her to do the same. She couldn't help but notice his frown, though that wasn't what bothered her the most. What set her on high alert was the too-careful-to-be-causal way he looked around the parking lot.

She did the same, trying to determine whether anything looked out of the ordinary. "What?" she finally asked.

Based on his expression, he was upset or angry. A hint of fear seemed to be present as well, but she couldn't say with great certainty.

"Knox called," he said.

Her stomach twisted tighter because there was only one reason for Knox to call while they were on the way to the hotel instead of simply waiting for Kipling to make it back home.

"So soon?" she asked.

"Yes."

"That was fast."

He nodded. "As it turns out, there is only one business in the US that has imported those roses recently."

"Who?" she asked, even though, deep inside, she knew what the answer would be.

"Finition Noire."

She forced herself to breathe normally. *In. Out. In. Out.*

"Are you okay?" he asked after about three more breaths.

She wasn't ready to talk yet, so she kept breathing in and out. At the same time, she tried to determine why it seemed like everything she did was somehow connected to the Benedicts.

"Alyssa," he said, more forcefully the second time. "Are you okay?"

Chapter Eight

Alyssa peeked at him with one eye, and Kipling wondered why he kept asking if she was okay when it was obvious she was not.

"No," she said. "Let me take a few more deep breaths, and then we'll reassess."

Kipling glanced around the parking lot again. He wasn't sure why, but something felt off. Almost as if they were being watched, but he didn't see how that was possible.

Unless…

He glanced at Alyssa. He didn't want to put additional stress on her, but he didn't want her out in the open if there were a potential threat nearby.

Her eyes were open, and all traces of fear were gone, replaced by an unwavering resolve. "We need to go."

"Why?"

Her gaze swept the parking lot. "I called the hotel earlier this afternoon, before I drove to Benedict House, to tell them I might come by tonight and to make sure they weren't booked. I never said for certain, but something doesn't feel right."

Since he had the same feeling, he couldn't agree more. He held out a hand. "Give me your keys. I'll call and have Knox come and get your car."

She stuck her hand in her pocket and handed over her keys. He collected her bag and settled her into the front seat. Within seconds they were headed south.

They weren't too far out of the city when a glance to his side showed him that her resolve was still in place. She amazed him with the way she handled everything.

"Where are we going?" she asked, catching the glance.

"Just a little way outside the city, where no one would expect us to be."

"You keep saying 'we'... Aren't you going back home?"

She'd asked the question with no emotion or any way for him to guess her preferred reply. He decided to answer with the same type of tone. "Not anymore."

"I should give you my credit card number." She bent down and reached for her purse, but he put a hand on her knee to stop her.

"No," he said. "This is on me. Remember? My contribution to the case."

"That was supposed to be things other than travel."

"I don't remember that stipulation."

"I just added it."

He smiled. It was a good sign she felt the need to argue. "It doesn't work that way."

"I'll let you pay this time," she said. "But don't take it as precedence."

"That's very magnanimous of you."

"Don't get used to it."

"I'll make a note of that." He couldn't hide the grin the brief exchange left on his face.

Her phone rang. "It's the lab."

"It's almost seven. Why would anyone be calling this late?"

"I sent an email earlier to see when I could expect results from Jade's hair." She answered the phone. "Hello?"

There was nothing but silence for a minute. Whatever she was told, it couldn't have been good news.

"No, I don't want anything preliminary. Let me know when you have something concrete." She ended the conversation with a curse.

"Problems?" Kipling asked.

"They told me it normally would have been finished and reported by now, which is why I sent an email in the first place, but it has to be repeated."

"Is that a good thing or a bad thing?"

"A test might have to be repeated for any number of reasons. Only some of them are because of the result."

Kipling drove the rest of the way in silence. Several minutes later, he pulled into a hotel's parking lot and retrieved Alyssa's bags. Of course, he didn't have anything other than the clothes he had on, but he'd deal with that later.

They walked together to the front desk and approached a woman who was much too perky for the time of day. Her chipper demeanor seemed especially obnoxious in light of everything that had happened in the past few hours.

"Yes, sir," she said before they'd even made it to the desk. "How can I help you?"

Kipling waited until he stood in front of her before answering. "We need two interconnecting suites and at least one them needs to have a large table. Put us down for a week, but we might end up extending."

Five minutes later, Kipling decided he didn't mind perky if it came with results like the front desk had arranged. The two suites were perfect. One had a conference table, and the other, a small kitchen.

But a glance at Alyssa showed her frowning.

"What?" Kipling asked.

"A week, maybe longer?" The frown deepened. "Why?"

"Everything we turn up points to whatever happened to your sister somehow being connected to whatever or whoever is threatening my family now. When I look at what happened to Tilly and Bea, I can picture something just as dangerous, if not more, happening to you."

She didn't let him finish. "You're forgetting that Knox and Bea were married and Keaton and Tilly were not only dating but also had an entire history of childhood memories together."

"I'm not forgetting anything, Alyssa. Whether you like it or not, you and I have been paired together."

"Because we danced at your brother's wedding?"

He walked across the room to stand in front of her, purposely getting inside her personal space but not touching her. She was a tall woman, but he was taller, and standing the way he was, she had no choice but to look up at him. "Tell me you don't feel the connection between us. Tell me your heart isn't racing right this very second." He ran a finger down her cheek. "Tell me you aren't affected in any way from my touch. That your body doesn't long for more. Tell me that, Alyssa, and I'll walk out of here and never bother you again."

She kept her eyes on him. "You know I can't."

He had no intention of gloating over her acquiescence. He wanted to kiss her. Badly. Standing as they were, he could feel her warmth, smell her delicate scent, and he wanted nothing more than to taste her.

But he wouldn't. At least for the moment. With a heavy

sigh, he forced himself to take a step backward and put some distance between them. "I'll do whatever it takes to keep you and my family safe. And if that means keeping a few hotel rooms for a week or so, that's what I'll do. Are you tired?"

For just a second, he sensed rather than saw her put her guard down. For that brief moment, it was as if he connected with the real Alyssa. Just a glimpse, but it was enough. Enough for him to know he would do anything to see more of that side of her.

"Not in any way, shape, or form."

"Me either." He nodded to the suite with the kitchen. "I'm going to go take what few things I have into the other room. Why don't you take some time to settle in, and we'll meet at your table in thirty minutes?"

"What are you going to do?"

"I'm going to call Knox and fill him in on where we are and make sure he's uploaded everything he has on Finition Noire to a secure and private server I have access to."

She cocked an eyebrow up. "Because you just happen to take your laptop wherever you go?"

He knew she had hers, but then again, she'd been planning to spend the night away. "No," he admitted. "But I never go anywhere without my tablet."

"If I didn't know better, I'd think you planned this."

"I would never do anything to intentionally scare you."

"I know that," she replied softly.

He simply smiled and said, "Back here in thirty?"

Chapter Nine

Alyssa groaned and pushed away from the table with a glance at her watch. "Ugh. We've been sitting here going through these records for hours. I need a break."

She'd taken a quick shower earlier, before they'd reconvened at the table. Kipling had somehow managed to change clothes. She wasn't sure if he just happened to keep extra in his car, along with his tablet, or if he'd called someone and had them sent over. She knew he'd had food delivered because, for the past few hours, they'd been snacking on delicious cheese cubes and crackers that tasted far too good to have come from a hotel vending machine.

She stood, lifting her hands high in the air, swallowing the moan from how good it felt to stretch. Expecting to find Kipling staring at her ass, she was surprised to see him stretching as well and couldn't help but appreciate the way his muscles moved under his shirt.

She remembered how his arms had felt wrapped around her at the wedding. How safe she'd felt, wrapped in their strength. Their gazes locked together, and for a second, something deliciously sinful passed between them.

"There's a bottle of wine in the other room, if you'd like a glass," he said, breaking the spell. "I know I could go for one."

"That sounds wonderful."

They walked silently into the living area of his suite, and she sat down on the couch while he gathered the glasses, the bottle, and a corkscrew.

"It's a red," he said. "I hope that's okay."

"It's wine. There's no way it could be anything other than okay." She gave the label a quick look as he uncorked the bottle. She wasn't a wine expert by any stretch but doubted the vintage was normally stocked by the hotel.

He gave a little laugh as he poured two glasses. "Don't be so sure. I've had plenty of awful wine in my time."

"I had wine out of a box a few years ago." She scooted over, giving him room to sit down beside her. "It wasn't as bad as I thought it would be."

He grimaced. "Why would you drink wine from a box?"

"Someone at the office gave it to Mac." She peeked at him to see if there was any judgment in his expression and found nothing. "The wine was way before..." She trailed off, not wanting to finish her sentence. "I'm sorry. I never quite know how to talk about him."

"How long were you two together?" he asked.

"Three years." Like she always did when Mac crossed her mind, she wondered how she could have been so blind.

Kipling gave a low whistle. "That's not an insignificant period of time."

"I know. I should have seen he was off long before I did."

"Why would you?"

She didn't understand his question. Or, more to the point, she didn't see the reason for the question.

"Hear me out." Kipling sounded so genuine, she found herself agreeing. "He basically led a double life you knew nothing about or had reason to suspect—I assume because he went to great lengths to keep it that way."

She had no trouble agreeing to that much.

"So what, in your opinion, was the clue you should have seen?" he asked.

She'd asked herself that too many times to count. Had played back, in her mind, conversations, interactions, anything. But nothing ever stood out as off or out of place.

"I don't know," she finally admitted. "But surely there was something. I knew he had gambling debt, but a lot of people do. There must have been something I missed."

"Why?"

"Because he was so evil, he had no business being around people. That kind of evil should be easy to spot."

"Should be. That doesn't mean it is," he spoke softly, keeping his eyes on her as if he could somehow look into her soul and speak to it directly. "Isn't that what makes evil horrific? The ability to masquerade as normal?"

She took a deep breath. "Somewhere inside, I know you're right. But that knowledge doesn't alleviate my guilt."

"The guilt you feel is personal. No one else holds you accountable. But you have to forgive yourself and move on. You're too good of a person to be alone forever because someone you had no control over did something horrible."

Neither of them spoke for a long moment, until she broke the silence again. "You're a tantalizing catch... Why hasn't someone taken you off the market?"

"You ask that as if to imply I'm willing to be taken off the market."

"Aren't you? I mean you're probably considered American royalty. Isn't it your job to produce an heir or two?" she asked in a joking, lighthearted manner. Yes, she wanted to know, but couldn't they discuss something with a touch of levity? Sometimes it felt like everything they talked about was shrouded in darkness and shadows.

He laughed. The abrupt change in the conversational tone had worked. "I suppose it is, but fortunately, I have two younger brothers, and one is married and the other engaged. I don't think producing an heir or two will be problematic for either couple."

"Leaving you as the perpetual bachelor?"

"I did want to settle down once," he talked with a faraway look and a heartbreakingly transparent expression. "I was a freshman in college and fell madly in love. I know it sounds ridiculous and clichéd, but what I felt for her was like nothing I'd experienced before."

Something in his voice made her heart hurt, and she wanted nothing more than to track this woman down and ask her what the hell she'd done to Kipling. "What happened?"

"I thought I was in love, and when she started asking for money, I gave and gave because I felt like it was my duty to take care of her. Hell, I brought her home to meet my family. They tried to warn me, and I refused to listen. Eventually, though, it became too much. When I stopped paying her bills, she got ugly. Talk mostly. But the gossip eventually made its way here. When I went home for the next break, Dad called me into his office as soon as I arrived. Our family lawyer, Derrick, was there, and he and Dad discussed filing a libel suit. I begged him not to. The way I saw it, it was only talk, and a suit would totally devastate her: financially, socially, you name it. I couldn't do that to her. Derrick ended up sending her a letter, and thankfully, everything stopped."

Alyssa nodded. "Let me guess. She told you that if you loved her you'd do it, right? A phrase used by all the best manipulators. It doesn't even matter what 'it' is. Their only real goal is to get you to do what they want you to do. To control you. It has nothing to do with love. Real love doesn't make ultimatums or demand proof."

"What about him?" Kipling asked with the relief of someone who'd just found a kindred spirit. "What did he want you to do?"

She could still hear Mac's voice, still recalled his round-about way of talking to her. "He wanted me to leave the police force. I later learned he didn't think women should be in law enforcement."

Kipling whistled low. "Wow."

She shivered. "Something in me knew not to marry him. At least I did something right."

"You've done a lot of things right," Kipling assured her. "I can't believe he'd want you to step away, knowing how good you are at your job and, especially, with what happened to your sister."

She jerked her head up. "He didn't know about my sister."

"That you had one or that she was murdered?"

"Either. He didn't know I had a sister, much less that she was killed."

Kipling didn't say anything, even though the question stayed in the room with them: *You told me but not your boyfriend of three years about your sister?*

He ran his hand through his hair. "I don't know about you, but my situation fucked me up. To this day, I rarely allow myself to see or go out with the same woman twice."

She raised an eyebrow.

"Present company excluded," he clarified.

"Why is that?"

"Damned if I know."

"Probably because we're not going out."

"I don't think that's it. I feel...safe around you." His eyes grew dark. "Though why that is, I'm not sure. *Safe* is definitely not the first word I think of when I'm around you. Not from the very first time I saw you." He shifted closer to her. "It was that day in Tilly's apartment. Do you remember? You were there with your partner."

He was so close, every so often she would catch a hint of the soap he washed with. Cedar with a hint of pine and something else she couldn't quite put her finger on. God, he smelled so good. She wanted to lick him.

"Don't let me stop you," he said.

"Damn it, did I say that out loud?" she asked. "It must be the wine. I'm usually in better control of myself."

"Note to self," he said. "Keep wine away from Alyssa."

She snorted. "Most guys would pour me more."

"I've seen far too many men take inappropriate liberties with women. I refuse to do so."

There was still a touch of sadness in his voice when he spoke, and she wished she knew how to make it go away.

She lifted a hand and lightly brushed his jaw, felt the stubble under her fingers. "You're one of the good guys, Kipling Benedict. You can fool some people, but you can't fool me. Under that gruff, take-no-prisoners exterior you show the world is a noble gentleman."

He turned his face to softly brush his lips across the palm of her hand. "I'm happy you think so. Once upon a time, I may have believed you, but now I'm not so sure."

The spot he kissed on her hand felt electrified, and she fought the overwhelming urge to ask him to do it again.

She focused on what he'd said. "That's okay. You don't

have to believe me right now. It's the truth, and you can't hide the truth, no matter if it's good or bad. You'll see it for yourself one day."

"Thank you. Listening to you, I almost believe it myself."

She cocked an eyebrow at him and dropped her hand. It was clear he wasn't going to kiss it again. "Why are you being so nice to me?"

He actually smiled, and it looked real this time. "What an odd question. Would you prefer I be boorish and rude?"

"What I'd prefer is for you to kiss me. And not on the hand this time."

A huge grin covered his face, and she groaned.

"I can't believe I said that out loud." And whether it was the wine or that she was just damn tired of denying what she wanted, she added, "But I can't deny the truth of it."

He nodded. "Then the way I see it," he said, "I can either pretend like I didn't hear you or..." He scooted closer, maddeningly close, but didn't touch her.

"Or?" she asked, shifting the last of the remaining distance between them, so close he could probably see her shirt move with the pounding of her heart. So close the side of his leg pressed against hers, yet it wasn't close enough.

He slowly raised his hand, all the while looking into her eyes, until he gently cupped her face. He stroked her cheek, and she shivered in response. "Or I could do this."

Her eyes drifted closed as his lips came toward her, and when they brushed hers, she feared she imagined it. She put her arms around him and drew him in for a longer kiss.

The moment their lips touched for a second time, Kipling groaned low in his throat and tightened his embrace. She feared he'd be hesitant, that maybe he hadn't wanted to kiss her, but any such thought was soon swept away as his lips crushed hers.

His fingers fisted her hair, holding her to him as he parted her lips and his tongue brushed hers. His other hand drifted to her waist, locking her in place. It was an altogether possessive and controlling move, but she wanted more. She ran her fingers down his back, ensuring he felt her nails. His groan assured her he not only felt them but also enjoyed them. He deepened the kiss and shifted, allowing her to brush against his erection.

A sharp knock on the door made them both jump. She opened her mouth to tell him not to answer it, but he was already standing up.

"Damn it all to hell," he muttered as he strode across the room. "What?" he asked, throwing the door open.

A uniformed man stood outside with a room-service tray. "Room service." The man stepped inside and placed the tray on a nearby table.

"Wait a minute," Kipling said. "I didn't order room service. Did you?" He looked at Alyssa.

Her heart began to race. "No."

She mentally calculated where her gun was and how long it'd take her to get it in her hand. She'd had it on when they arrived but had taken it off before her shower. Which meant it now sat useless in her room. She cursed her stupidity.

Kipling jerked the paper with the order from the server. "This says room 1845. We're room 1945." He looked at Alyssa and nodded. *It's all okay*, he said, silently. *Just a misunderstanding.*

Despite the knowledge it was only a room mix-up, her body continued trembling even after the deliveryman apologized profusely and left. She walked with shaky legs into her adjourning room and strapped on her weapon, making sure it was loaded. They had been fortunate this time. She would not find herself unarmed again.

She'd been refusing to think about it, but now that it looked as if they might find out who was responsible for her sister's murder, she wondered if she would be able to find the courage to do what she had scarcely let herself imagine —leave the police department for good. When she'd left to help Kipling, she'd always intended to go back.

But what if she didn't?

It was a dream she only let herself contemplate at night, when she was all alone. That time when reality was shrouded in darkness and anything seemed possible. Those few precious moments when she danced between alertness and dreams, when she would allow herself to drift.

She'd always loved history, though she'd never given serious thought to what she'd do with a history degree. How could she when she'd decided at such a young age to become a cop? But at night, she allowed herself to imagine the possibilities.

She could be a history teacher. Or do research. Maybe work in a museum. Or maybe she'd go even further and get a degree in archaeology. Go abroad. She would usually chuckle as she thought about becoming the next Indiana Jones.

But as she stood in the room, it hit her. After they solved the case, she wouldn't have a reason to be around Kipling anymore. She looked to her side, and her heart sank. No matter how passionately he'd kissed her, she would always have her sister's death hanging over her. Even if she wanted to quit the police force for good, she doubted she could. How else would she be able to help other missing women and their families?

And as for Indiana Jones, although he always had a romance, it never seemed to work out. The same would hold true for her. No matter which way it turned out, history or police, at the end of the day, she would still be alone.

Kipling hadn't followed her into her room. Giving her privacy, she supposed.

It was probably a good thing the room service had been mistakenly delivered to his room, because if it hadn't, she wasn't sure she'd have been able to walk away from him.

Chapter Ten

The next day, Alyssa and Kipling worked separately. However, they didn't leave the hotel rooms and kept the door between their suites open so they were within eyesight of each other.

For his part, Kipling seemed to want to ignore the kiss they'd shared the night before.

Alyssa told herself she was being ridiculous. Even if Kipling wanted to discuss it, what was there to say other than they shouldn't do it again? If she were smart, she'd stop thinking about him, period.

Still, he got to her in little ways. How he'd pour her more coffee if he was getting himself some. The way he'd adjust the thermostat when he saw she was cold. He was exactly what she'd pegged him as the night before—a gentleman. Frankly, he'd been a lot easier to deal with when he was just an obnoxious rich guy she could write off as an asshole.

But now, sharing the suites, he was always nearby or underfoot. She could never *not* think about him. And though she tried not to let those thoughts drift toward the carnal, it didn't always work.

Late in the afternoon, an email appeared in her inbox. The sender and subject had her calling for Kipling. He made it to her side in less than five seconds.

"Everything okay?" he asked.

She turned to face him, blocking his view of the computer. "Yes, I wanted you to be here before I did anything else."

He tried to look over her shoulder. "Did you find something?"

"That's yet to be seen, but I got an email from the lab. It should be the report on Jade's hair."

"Thank goodness. I was beginning to think it would never show up."

She turned back around to face her laptop. "I was getting ready to log on to the portal and bring everything up. But I wanted you to be here to see."

He pulled a chair over to her side and sat down. "Go for it." While she was logging in, he asked, "Tell me again what you tested and what we could potentially see."

"From Jade's hair, we tested mitochondrial DNA. It's less specific because all the females in a family will have the exact same expression. So, if Jade's biological mother, sister, grandmother, or aunt is in the system, we'll find them. In this case, we're throwing our net wide in hopes of finding out more about Jade. Especially since we already know who her father is."

"Makes sense," Kipling said as she pulled up the home screen.

Alyssa typed in her username and password and held her breath as her account page loaded. She hadn't used this lab too many times in the past and hoped word of her leave of absence hadn't made it to the private lab. Fortunately, her account showed the handful of cases and tests she'd ordered in the past. At the top of the screen was Jade's test file marked as completed with a hyperlink to the report.

"Does that mean there was a match?" Kipling asked. "Or would they still use a hyperlink to tell us there was no match found?"

"Good question," Alyssa said. She clicked on the hyperlink, but instead of getting results, she was taken to another account-verification page. "Are you kidding me with this?" she asked no one in particular.

"What?" Kipling asked. "Does it normally not do that?"

"It's never done it to me before." She went through her security questions to verify who she was before the system allowed her to continue. "Very interesting. I don't know if it's a new layer of security or if it's because the results are sensitive."

She hadn't thought about that angle. What if Jade's mother wasn't dead but was a celebrity? Knowing what she did of Franklin Benedict, she could see it happening.

It became such a tempting possibility in her mind that she was pondering who the celebrity could be when the report populated her screen.

"What does it say?" Kipling asked.

She read the summary. It didn't make any sense at all, so she read it a second time. The second read through was worse than the first. She refreshed her screen. Her body must have processed the results faster than her brain because her hand trembled in shock.

"Alyssa?" Kipling asked again.

She clicked on the report. The summary must have been wrong, that was all there was to it.

"Damn it," Kipling nearly growled. "Tell me what's wrong. I've never seen you like this before."

She couldn't talk to him yet. She had to know. If she was going to tell him what the results indicated, she had to believe two hundred percent that there could be no mistake. Taking a deep breath, she read through the words on the screen, from the first sentence that started with the date of the sample to the last sentence that simply stated, "Results verified by repeat analysis."

Satisfied, at least intellectually, she turned to Kipling. He sat completely still. His expression showed he knew something bad was getting ready to happen, but there was a lingering hint of hope that he was wrong. He wasn't, though.

She took a deep breath. "Jade's sample hit on three profiles in the nationwide database."

"Really?" he asked, and there was that damn hope again. More pronounced this time. "Three? That's really good news, isn't it?"

Damn, but it was hard to talk, sitting in front of him the way she was. The best thing she could do was spit it out. All at once. "The three matching profiles are me, my sister, and my mother."

He sat frozen for several long seconds.

"You?" he finally asked in a hoarse voice. "Why are you a match?"

"Jade is either my half sister or my niece. I'm inclined to go with my niece because the timing fits and I'm fairly certain I'd remember my mom being pregnant. I don't believe any teenager can be so self-absorbed as to not notice that."

"Your sister?" he asked.

"Yes."

He hung his head and buried his hands in his hair. All at once, he sat up, eyes blazing, but she wasn't sure with what exactly. "Your murdered sister."

King

King's house
Charleston, South Carolina

"Sir?" King's butler knocked on the door.

King stood, panting, as he looked over the pile of glass, water, and leather that had once been on his desk. Somewhere in the background, Alyssa and Kipling kept talking, thanks to the bugging device he'd planted.

"Go away!" King yelled.

"But, sir—"

"Go. Away."

His wife had given him a rare fifteenth-century Ming vase for their anniversary not long after they'd married. The antique blue-and-white porcelain made a satisfying smash as his fist connected and it shattered to the floor.

The butler, wisely, was silent.

How had he missed the fact that Allison and Alyssa were sisters? How? They didn't even have the same last name.

But they would die the same way. He smiled, wondering if Alyssa would sound just as pathetic begging for her life as her sister had in the seconds before he slit her throat.

Chapter Eleven

"Now we know what the connection is between our families," Kipling said.

"We know your father slept with my sister when she was barely eighteen," Alyssa countered. "And we know he got her pregnant. It still doesn't make sense. We don't know where she went for five years or why she came back. We don't know who killed her or why. We don't know who Jade's guardian is. And we still don't have a clue who or what Finition Noire is. We don't know anything."

"I disagree. We actually know a bit more than that," Kipling said, risking her wrath, and, not surprisingly, she glared at him. "Listen to me. I believe we now have a good understanding as to why your stepfather kicked her out of the house. He found out she was pregnant. And I would be willing to bet that's the same reason he kicked her out again when she returned five years later."

Kipling hadn't been able to wrap his head around the lab report. How was it possible his father had slept with such a young girl? That he got her pregnant and did nothing to support either her or his child? He wouldn't have thought his father to be so cold, so uncaring, but there it was.

Alyssa stood up. "I have to get out of here. Walk. Do something. I don't care what, I have to get out of this hotel room."

"I'll go with you," Kipling said.

"You don't have to."

"I know I don't, but I want to. And I don't want you to be by yourself. It's not safe."

She didn't argue but calmly walked to the door and waited for him to get ready.

Of course, once they were outside, he saw what her plan was. She took off, walking quickly, not looking behind to make sure he followed her or talking to him at all.

He knew she had received quite a shock today. Hell, he had too.

After walking about four blocks, she finally turned. "I wish one of them were here," she said. "I don't care which one. I'd ask them what the hell they thought they were doing. And if they had any idea how much they would mess up everything because of their actions. I want to ask Allison if it was worth it." Tears filled her eyes. "And then it hits me, I can't, because she's dead. And regardless of what she would say, it wasn't worth it at all."

He moved toward her, unsure how she would react but knowing he had to do something. He placed a tentative hand on her shoulder, and when she didn't flinch or try to move away, he placed one on the other. She took a step toward him, and he enveloped her in his arms. For several minutes, he held her, and though he meant to give her comfort, she gave him the same.

"Let's go back to the hotel and regroup." He kept an

arm around her and gently turned her back to the hotel. "We need to plan our next steps."

She didn't say anything, and silently, they walked back to the hotel together.

Alyssa knew as soon as she entered her suite that someone had been in her room, and it hadn't been housekeeping. Kipling had placed the DO NOT DISTURB signs on their doors before they went out. Not to mention her bed was still unmade and the towels unchanged.

There was nothing she could point to as proof. Rather, it was a feeling in her gut. Those who had never experienced it would likely not understand, but after years of working on the police force, she'd learned to listen when her gut spoke.

She took her weapon and carefully looked over everything, searching for any tiny detail to back up her feeling. Nothing was out of place until she reached the work area. In the middle of the conference table, a kitchen knife had been shoved into the tabletop, pinning a picture to the surface. She gasped when she saw what it was.

The crime-scene photo of her sister's body.

To the side was a typed note: *Your sister couldn't stay away from Benedict men, either. You'd better learn or else you'll meet the same fate.*

She hadn't realized she was shaking until she tried to take a step forward and almost fell. She reached for the knife, then stopped herself. It was unlikely the culprit left fingerprints, but on the off chance they hadn't wiped the knife handle, she was going to dust it for prints.

"Kipling," she called. "Come here, please."

She blocked out the picture of her sister's broken body as best as she could and tried to concentrate on the note.

She had the feeling there was something she needed to pay attention to, outside of the words on the note.

Kipling's footsteps sounded, getting louder as he came closer. "Alyssa?"

She didn't answer. All her focus was concentrated on the note. There was something there. What was it she was missing?

"What's wrong?" Kipling stood in the doorway and then, seeing her, walked over and put his arms around her.

She pointed at the table. Because she couldn't look at the picture again, she kept her focus on Kipling's face and watched as his shock turned to rage.

"What the hell is this?" he asked.

Alyssa collapsed into a nearby chair. "That's my sister. Or was."

He looked down at the picture once more and cursed under his breath. "Who did this?"

She assumed he meant the picture and the knife since they both knew she had no idea who had murdered her sister. "I don't know. They must have slipped in here while we were out." She shivered at the thought. God, that had been close. Following along that line of thought, she decided enough was enough. The time had come to take these bastards down once and for all.

* * *

THERE WERE TOO many emotions going through Kipling's body at the moment. Rage. Shock. Disgust. Fear.

"How did they know?" he asked. "Seriously. How? I mean, we just found out. And unless I'm mistaken, those reports are confidential. Right?"

She nodded, but her attention seemed to be elsewhere

and no longer focused on him or the knife in the middle of the table.

"Alyssa?" he asked as she walked away from the table.

She looked at him only to hold her finger to her mouth. He raised an eyebrow. She wanted him to be quiet? What was her deal? Who could they possibly be disturbing?

It hit him as she moved around the room, running her hand under the various surfaces. He told himself it was only a precaution and one they should have taken before now. But when she stopped in front of the table the deliveryman had used the night before to set the room-service tray down, Kipling knew it was more than a mere formality. She looked resigned, sighed deeply, and pointed to a bug.

Fucking hell. Kipling frantically tried to remember everything they had discussed since. So damn much.

They needed to get out of the hotel, and quickly. The only thing was, he wasn't sure where they could go. Alyssa was one step ahead of him, pulling papers together and packing them up. She motioned with her fingers for him to go get his stuff.

"I'm hungry," she said like it was the most natural thing in the world. He was once more struck by her calmness and how she always acted so cool under pressure. "Do you think you could eat dinner early?"

"I don't see why not. I'd love a big ole rack of ribs." He grinned at the last part, knowing Alyssa didn't eat pork.

She stuck her tongue out at him. "Why do we always have to get what you want?" she asked. "Why don't I get to choose for once?"

They continued their fake argument as they went around the room, throwing their clothes and toiletries in whichever bag was the closest. By the time they decided where they were going to go for dinner, they were packed.

From the conversation they'd had, no one would have guessed they walked out of the two suites with no intention of ever returning. By silent agreement, neither one of them said anything until they made it to Kipling's car. Alyssa did a quick check, looking for both GPS devices and bugs but finding neither.

"We lucked out," she said as they climbed into his car. "They weren't expecting you, so nothing of yours is bugged. We have to be more careful from now on. I can't believe I didn't think to look for bugs after that bogus deliveryman last night."

She almost added she didn't know where her head had been, but she knew the answer to that one. It had been on Kipling and his kiss.

"Hopefully, that'll keep them off our trail for a bit," Alyssa said as Kipling sped away from the hotel as quickly as he could without drawing attention. "We need a place to stay that whoever is looking for us won't find easily."

"I've been thinking along those lines," Kipling said. "I think I have the perfect place."

"Where?" Alyssa asked, as if she found it hard to believe he'd have the perfect location at his fingertips.

"We own a beach place down in Edisto," he said. "It's in my mother's maiden name, so someone would have to look hard and dig deep to find it."

"It sounds perfect. But why is it in your mother's maiden name?"

"My grandparents, my mother's parents, were never thrilled with my mom marrying my dad. You have to understand, at least from their point of view, Franklin Benedict wasn't to be trusted. You think my brothers and I are given a hard time by the press? Apparently, compared to my father, all three of us qualify for sainthood."

"Their opinion didn't change after your parents got married?"

Kipling grimaced. He wasn't one to share dirty family secrets, but Alyssa's sister had not only slept with his father but had also borne him a child. But more than that, he wanted to share things about his family with her. He wanted her in their inner circle. "The thing is," he told her, "I was born six months after their wedding and weighed almost nine pounds."

"Oh, man," Alyssa said.

"Right? There was no way they could pass me off as early." He shrugged. "I'm not sure if that was their plan or not. Either way, my mom's parents never got along with my dad."

"Are they still around?"

"They are, but they're in France and only make it stateside about once every three years. They say the air in France keeps them young, and they're both almost ninety. Who am I to argue with that?"

"They sound like they're quite the pair."

Kipling couldn't help but smile. "They are. I do wish I was able to see them more. I swear, they're busier than most people half their age. My grandmother has the ear of a few fashion designers. Last time we saw her, she had just given her opinion on fashion accessories for the mature woman. There was a purse strap she said was going to revolutionize the industry." He chuckled. "I remember her exasperation that her three grandsons didn't understand what made it so wonderful. She mumbled something about testosterone and went to find Maggie, saying she would better appreciate her brilliance."

He glanced to his side, expecting to see Alyssa grin at

the story, but instead he found himself unable to read her expression. "Are you okay?"

"Her purse," she said. "My sister's purse. That's what's missing in the crime-scene photo."

"What do you mean, missing?"

"Her purse was in the box of things the police brought over, but it wasn't in the crime-scene photo."

"Tell me what I'm missing, Alyssa," he said. "Tell me why the purse should have been in the photo."

She took a deep breath. "She never went anywhere without that purse, and in the photo, she was dressed to go out. The purse should have been by her side, but it wasn't. I remember seeing the purse in the box when they brought it to Mom. I couldn't believe Allison had been carrying it for five years."

She didn't say anything else, and Kipling glanced to his side. "What?"

"I can't believe I didn't realize it sooner. I gave her that purse for her birthday. I was in Scouts and had learned how to add a secret compartment. Oh my god. I forgot! She used to joke she could hide the secrets of the whole world in there. What she really meant, though, were things she didn't want Mom to see. Notes from boys, that sort of thing."

"Is it possible whoever found the purse also discovered the secret compartment? Maybe emptied it of anything possibly incriminating?"

"Entirely possible," she said. "Whatever Allison hid in the purse, if anything, I'm sure is gone by now."

He pulled into the driveway of the beach house, but instead of heading to the main house, he took a small side drive and came to a stop at a much smaller property.

Kipling turned to her. "This cottage was added when

we were kids. On the off chance someone does know about the main property, even fewer people know about this place."

Her halfhearted nod and faraway expression told him her body was with him but her mind was still thinking about a purse. From the times he'd worked with her, he knew she was very thorough and would never leave any clue unexamined.

"Alyssa?" he asked softly, placing a hand on top of hers. "I agree with you. We need to get the purse and make sure there's nothing in it."

She looked at him in surprise. "But I didn't say anything."

"Not with your mouth, you didn't." It took all his strength not to brush her lips with his own. "I vote we get settled inside. Then you can look at the picture again, and I'll call Knox."

"To see if he can find out anything about the purse?"

He shook his head. "To find out who became Jade's guardian after your sister's death."

Chapter Twelve

They walked into the cottage, and Kipling pointed to the outside patio where he suggested she sit and look over the photo while he ensured the house was ready for occupancy.

It didn't take Alyssa long to review the photo, just long enough to verify that the purse was the only item she had a question about.

She leaned back in the wicker rocker and watched as Kipling set about making sure the house would meet their needs for the next few days. Again it struck her how this giant of business and industry was just as comfortable setting up a cottage as he was running negotiations.

Her stomach rumbled, reminding her how long it'd been since they ate. She got up and wandered into the kitchen to see if she could find something to fix for dinner. She found what she was looking for right as Kipling came up behind her.

"Did you find anything?" he asked. "I was going to take a shower, but it can wait."

She shooed him out of the kitchen. "You. Out. Go get a shower. I can handle dinner."

Once he was out of the kitchen, she pulled out the shrimp she'd found in the freezer and grabbed the grits she'd discovered in the pantry. She didn't cook a lot but considered shrimp and grits one of her specialties. Within minutes, she had the shrimp thawing and the sauce cooking. By the time Kipling rejoined her, everything was coming along nicely.

"If that's shrimp and grits I smell," he said, coming up behind her to peek over her shoulder, "I'm yours forever."

"You may want to wait until you've tasted it."

"Nah," he said. "I can tell by the smell it's going to be great."

She didn't say anything but turned around to face him so she could see his expression when she came back with a snappy reply. However, when she turned around, she found he was in her personal space, close enough for her to smell the soap from his recent shower. She forgot everything she was going to say and do.

"Yes?" he asked, a hint of laughter in his voice.

"I had to do the grits a different way. They might not be good." She didn't know why she told him that, other than it was the only thing she could think of to say that didn't involve his being naked and wet.

She ducked around him and grabbed the two plates she'd set out earlier. Kipling took them from her with an, "Allow me," and carried them out to the small table on the patio.

Flustered and hating herself for feeling that way, she snatched up the napkins and forks and followed. She didn't know why she felt so out of sorts, but when she made it to the patio and found him holding one of the chairs out for her, the out-of-sorts feeling slipped away. At the sight of his easy smile and breezy confidence, she couldn't help but feel the same.

"I hope this table will do, ma'am," he said seriously, as if he was indeed working in an upscale restaurant and not standing on his family's patio. "I'm afraid we're rather busy tonight and this is all we have available." His composure slipped on the last sentence, and he coughed in what she assumed was an attempt to cover up a chuckle.

Playing along, she slipped into the offered seat with a sigh. "I suppose I'm not in any position to complain since I didn't have the courtesy to call ahead."

He nodded and turned away, doing something she couldn't see. When he turned back around, he had what appeared to be a wine bottle in his hand. He held it out as if allowing her to inspect its label.

"Ma'am?" he asked.

He still had the playful grin on his face, but she couldn't imagine why. However, when he took a step closer, she saw it wasn't a wine bottle at all but rather a plain glass decanter, and she swallowed a laugh.

"South Carolina. Lowcountry. Current year, flat," he said, his grin getting bigger. "It's our best reserve yet. I thought, considering what happened the last time I gave you wine, water might be the best choice tonight."

She didn't try to swallow her laugh this time; she let it out, waving at his seat across from her as she did so. "Please," she said between laughs, "sit down."

He finally relented, taking the seat across from her with a sigh. "I could never work in the service industry."

She raised an eyebrow. "Was I really that bad? I thought I was very polite."

"It's not you," he assured her. "I was just thinking about

how it could be." He poured himself a glass of water and sat back to take a long sip. "I probably wouldn't last one night. More than likely, I'd end up punching someone. Or cussing them out. Either way, it wouldn't be pretty, and I'd end up getting myself fired."

"All that aside, I think you did a fine job out here on your parents' patio. In fact, I thought I might set up a reservation for tomorrow night." She twirled her water-filled wineglass. "I thought the service was exemplary."

"If you think dinner service is good, you should see this place at breakfast."

There was nothing inherently suggestive about his statement. After all, they had shared several breakfasts together over the past few days and none had been remotely uncomfortable. So why was her face heated and her heart racing at his statement?

Because there were hours to go until breakfast, and his intense look led her to believe he had several suggestions about how they could spend them. Quite a change from what she'd thought he felt as early as a month ago when she couldn't picture him with a police officer.

But no sooner had that thought popped into her mind than she chastised herself for being so rude and disrespectful to Kipling in her thoughts. She had never—not before they wound up together like they currently were or over the past few days—seen him hold himself above or look down on anyone.

Kipling Benedict was not a snob. If anyone was being judgmental about class or a bank-account balance, it was her. The realization made her feel very small. Was she really so petty she wouldn't want Kipling because he was wealthy?

She recalled his words from the not-so-distant past, one of the first times they'd met.

"For the record, I'm not just wealthy. I'm insanely wealthy. And guess what? News flash. Everyone is for sale. Even you. All I have to do is find your price. Would you like for me to try? Rumor has it I'm very thorough when it comes to something I want to buy."

She realized his words now for what they truly were—a defense mechanism designed to keep him from getting hurt. If he could make the world think he was nothing more than a playboy, then no one would bother to get to know him. And that way, he would never get hurt.

He sat across the table from her, serving them both hearty scoops of grits followed by the shrimp she'd made to go on top. He caught her looking and smiled, but it wasn't until he frowned that she realized she hadn't smiled back.

"Are you not hungry?" he asked, and she knew she had been a fool.

Who had hurt him so much he no longer wanted anyone to get close to him? It had to be the girl from college he'd told her about. It was a good thing Alyssa wasn't around in those days; she'd have taught that piece of trash a thing or two.

"Alyssa?" he asked, this time with concern in his voice because she'd never replied.

"I'm good," she said.

"Are you sure? You looked confused there a few seconds ago."

"That was nothing. Just me hoping dinner doesn't suck." She picked up her fork. "Eat up."

Chapter Thirteen

"I don't believe you for a minute," Kipling told her. Though, normally, if she didn't want to tell him something, no amount of badgering would get her to change her mind, he decided to try. "Tell me."

She put her fork down with a sigh. "If you must know, I was thinking about that girl from your college days and how I wished I knew who she was, because I'd love to tell her a thing or two. Can we change the topic now?"

He wasn't sure she realized how much her response touched him. Without a thought of teasing or pushing her buttons for a response, he did as she asked and changed the topic completely, immediately launching into stories of his childhood when the Benedict clan came to their beach property.

He told her about a sea turtle Keaton wanted to take home to Benedict House and how his youngest brother had concocted a story about the turtle coming up to the beach house while everyone else slept. Keaton would let him in, and together they'd drink orange soda and eat Maggie's chocolate chip cookies.

Kipling leaned in close. "Maggie told him that, if she woke up and found a sea turtle had eaten her cookies and tracked sand in all over the floors she'd cleaned, she'd never make cookies for him again. Knox jumped up and said no turtle was going to eat his cookies. He was going to go to the beach, capturing that turtle, and making soup out of it."

Alyssa laughed softly. The first time she'd done so all evening. "How did Keaton take that?"

It hit him that, with her family situation being what it was, she probably didn't have many stories to share about her sister. "Alyssa, I'm so sorry." He shook his head. "I never meant... I mean, I go on and on all the time, and it never occurred to me to stop and think that you..."

He looked up, expecting to see her upset or possibly sad, but instead, the opposite was true. She looked serene, for lack of a better word. The late-evening light touched her hair in a way that almost made her appear to glow, or at least made her look otherworldly. He wasn't sure he'd ever be able to perfectly describe how she looked, but the effect was stunning. She was stunning. All at once, he found his mouth so dry, he couldn't speak.

Seemingly unaware, she ever so gently placed her hand on top of his. "You're worried about telling me about you and your brothers growing up because you know I don't have anything similar to share about my sister?"

He winced slightly and put down the glass of water he'd taken a sip from. "It made more sense in my head than it did to hear you say it out loud."

She didn't move her hand, and he swore he felt her touch echo throughout his body. "I can only imagine the way you grew up, with two brothers, makes my childhood look very boring and bleak. But I had fun. There were some good times too."

"I didn't mean to imply otherwise."

"I know you didn't."

She hadn't moved her hand. A quick glance at the table told him she had finished her dinner.

"Ah," he said. "I knew you were mistaken about something."

Her only response was an arched eyebrow. He loved how she used the perfectly sculpted brow to convey any number of sentiments. In the past, she'd lifted it at him in annoyance, in disbelief, and, like now, in question. He imagined the same brow had been lifted a time or two during her law-enforcement career as well.

"You're killing me with the eyebrow," he said.

"I'm waiting for you to tell me what I was mistaken about."

"The grits," he said. "You said you thought they would be awful, but they weren't. They were wonderful."

She glanced at his empty plate. "Or perhaps," she said, "you're a typical guy and will eat anything put in front of you."

He didn't answer for a few seconds, instead choosing to look at her and gaze into her eyes. When he finally answered, his voice was low and she had to lean forward to hear him. "Do you really think I'm a typical guy?"

This close to her, he could see she trembled. It wasn't cold, and she wasn't frightened. Which left one thing. Other than the kiss at the hotel, they'd ignored this thing between them for the most part. That stopped tonight.

"Do you, Alyssa?" he asked again.

She tried to jerk her hand back, but he wouldn't let her. He didn't hold it tightly, but gently. When she stopped trying to pull away, he brought it to his lips and placed a kiss on her knuckles.

"Do you?" he asked again.

"No."

No. That word said in answer to any other question at a point like this would've stopped him. But said in response to the question he'd asked, it pushed him forward.

"Thank you," he said. "I have to admit I'd be rather put out if you thought of me as typical. For the record, I don't think there's anything typical about you, either."

"Kipling," she said. "What are we doing?"

"At the moment, the only thing we're doing is talking. We're two people who just finished a delightful meal, and now we're sitting at the table, enjoying each other's company."

"That isn't what I meant."

He knew she was going to say that. It made a part of him, deep inside, very pleased with himself that he could predict her so well. "Then you must have asked the wrong question. Perhaps what you should have asked was, 'What are we going to do?' "

He might be pleased with his ability to guess what she would say next, but her laugh told him she knew him just as well.

"What?" he asked, though he had a feeling he didn't need to ask.

"As soon as the words left my mouth, I knew what you were going to say," she said.

"What am I getting ready to say now, Alyssa?"

She dipped her head, trying to hide the color his question brought to her cheeks, he assumed. "I don't know," she said.

He stood, and she looked up, but if she thought he was getting ready to leave the patio, she was sorely mistaken. He held his hand out, and she took it, rising to her feet.

He remained silent and waited for her to say something. She lifted her head and looked at him with such intensity he could no longer be quiet. "I want you, Alyssa."

Her eyes showed no surprise. "I know."

He appreciated she appeared neither embarrassed nor coy, but remained rather matter-of-fact about the entire thing. He had no idea it would be so refreshing for a woman to act that way.

"I know," she repeated. "And by now, you must know that I want you too."

"Yes," he said, with the same straightforwardness she had given him.

"But I'm not sure what I want to do about it."

He brought her hand to his lips and kissed her fingertips. "I sure as hell know what I want to do about it. Come to bed with me, Alyssa."

She closed her eyes. "I don't know."

"You do know." He brought her hand to his lips again but this time kissed her open palm and hid a smile when her eyes flew open.

"Yes," she admitted.

"Tell me what's making you hesitate."

"So you can tell me why I shouldn't feel that way?"

"So I can understand."

She took a deep breath and seemed to steel herself. "I'm afraid I'm going to like it too much."

"I would hope so," he couldn't stop himself from saying. "Otherwise, I'd consider myself a horrible failure."

"And," she continued as if he hadn't said anything, "I'm not sure I want to know it can be so good, if I can't be with you."

"Why wouldn't you be able to be with me?"

She tried to turn her head, but he took his free hand and held her in place, forcing her to meet his gaze.

"Tell me why you wouldn't be able to be with me," he stated again.

"Don't make me say it."

"I'm afraid you're going to have to say it, because I don't have any idea where you're going with this line of thinking."

"I'm a police officer. You're a Benedict."

He dropped her hand. "Damn it, Alyssa. Are we back to that again? Really?"

"Listen to me. You keep saying it doesn't matter, but it does. Bea is an attorney, her brother is one of the wealthiest men in the state. And sure, Tilly worked as a waitress in a gentlemen's club, but she was *born* wealthy. She's part of that lifestyle."

"I don't know what I can say or do to make you understand I don't give a damn about your net worth."

"You say that now, but one day it will matter." She held up her hand when he tried to speak. "Let me finish. I know you don't think so, but it will. Maybe not this month or even this year, but one day you'll see that you need a woman who can understand and fit into your world. A woman at ease with everything it holds. More importantly, you need a woman who won't be forever tainted by the choices of men she dated."

She was bringing Mac into this? Suddenly, he couldn't stand to hear it anymore. He dropped her hand. "If that's how you really feel about me, it looks like we're done here." He put on the frostiest expression he had. The one he always used when he needed to be a cold-hearted bastard. "I have to thank you for ensuring we didn't go any further. What a colossal mistake that would have been. Now, if you'll excuse me, I think I'll go for a walk. I'm too agitated to stay inside right now. Don't worry about the dishes, I'll take care of them when I get back. And don't wait up. I don't know how long I'll be out."

* * *

Alyssa watched as he turned and walked away. Not once did he look back at her. But then again, she didn't call out to him, either. She knew if she did, she'd take back everything she'd just said because, even if what she said was true, she didn't care. She wanted him. Wanted to be with him. And damn the consequences.

She took the dishes back inside the house, refusing to look down the hall where the bedrooms were. If she hadn't been such a complete and utter ass, they'd be headed down that hall right now, on the way to his bedroom.

"I royally fucked that up," she said to no one. The question was, why?

She thought as she washed the dishes and put them away. While she cleaned the pots she'd cooked with and set the patio table to rights, she thought even more.

When everything was in the exact location and in the same shape she'd found it, she ventured to the bedroom he'd put her stuff in and prepared to take a shower.

She had one shot to fix this mess. She wasn't going to screw it up.

It was two hours later before she heard the front door open. Darkness had fallen and, except for the one dim lamp she'd kept on in the living room, everything inside the house was dark. If he went by looks alone, he'd assume she'd taken his advice and gone to bed.

She loosened the belt around the robe she had on, preparing for him to make his way to where she was.

Closing her eyes, she took a deep breath and, seconds later, heard his steps enter the living room.

She knew exactly when he saw her because his breath hitched and he spoke, though in a lower voice than she'd thought he'd use.

"I thought I told you not to wait up," he said.

She stood up. "There are a few things I need to say."

"That's great. Unfortunately, those are things I have no interest in hearing."

He took a step toward the hall, but she moved faster and blocked his way.

"I was wrong," she said.

"I know you were."

He wasn't going to make any part of this easy on her, not that she expected him to, nor did she particularly want him to. He wouldn't believe her if she didn't fight for it.

"I was also scared."

He may have expected the first few things she said, but he had not planned on her saying that. His body tensed. "Scared of me?"

"No, of course not. Not you."

He seemed to realize he was stuck then. Since he'd questioned her on what she'd said, he could no longer plead disinterest, and she knew him well enough to know he would never be so impolite as to simply walk away. But that didn't mean he'd ask her another question.

Therefore, she took it upon herself to answer what he wouldn't ask. "I'm scared of what I feel for you. I'm scared because it's the most real and intense thing I've ever felt, and I was afraid if you knew exactly how much I felt, it'd scare you off and you'd want nothing to do with me. But the minute you walked out tonight, I knew I'd rather scare you with the truth than run you off with a lie."

He still didn't say anything. Nothing about him, not his stance or body language or expression, gave any insight into what he was feeling or thinking. She couldn't even guess if he'd be open to what she planned next.

This was it. He would either welcome her or reject her, but either way, they'd have closure. She lifted her head. "What I'd like is to have a do-over." Nothing but silence from him. Calling upon every bit of strength she could find in her body, she looked him in the eyes and repeated the part of the conversation where everything had gone wrong earlier. "Surely, by now you know I want you too."

He stood there and looked at her. The seconds went by, feeling like hours, and he only stood there.

She told herself she was not going to cry. She'd known it was a risk when she'd decided to wait for him. She'd been brave enough to roll the dice, and now she had to prove she was brave enough to lose.

She dropped her head and took a step back, vowing not to cry until she was alone.

"Yes."

He spoke it so low, she thought it was only in her head. She took another step back, and he said it again.

"Yes." This time he spoke louder. "I know you want me too."

She allowed herself to look up. Gone was his blank expression, and in its place were longing and desire and need. For her.

"And god knows I want you, Alyssa." It was all he had time to say because, as soon as he'd started talking, they both began walking toward each other, and when he said her name, they were already in each other's arms.

She lifted her head at the same time he lowered his, and at the touch of his lips on hers, she knew she'd redo all the uncertainty of the past few minutes, time and time again, to experience the heaven she found in his arms and in his kiss.

He pulled back only long enough to ask, "Bed?" and for her to reply, "God, yes," and then he took her face in his hands and kissed her again.

They made their way to his room in what had to be the most clumsy, disjointed walk ever, both of them trying to undress yet unwilling to separate from the other to do so. They somehow made it, though, and by the time they did, they'd managed to remove most of their clothing. Or, rather, she had managed to get hers off, since she'd only had a robe on. Kipling still had his T-shirt and boxer briefs.

She reached for them, but he shook his head.

"Why not?" she asked.

"Because this." He placed his hands on her shoulders and walked her backward until her legs bumped the bed. "Since you're already naked, I'm going to kiss you all over."

"I don't think I agreed to those rules," she said, just to see what he'd do.

"Give me five minutes and you'll agree to just about anything I suggest."

"Four," she countered with a playful grin, because really, he could take as long as he pleased to do anything he wanted.

"Alyssa, if I stop at four, the only thing that's going to happen is your begging for more."

She almost laughed and replied with a smart-ass remark, but before she could speak the first word, he'd lifted her onto the bed and placed her on her back. His mouth was on her neck and moving lower, and the only thoughts in her head were, *Yes*, and, *Please don't stop*. She tried speaking them, but what came out sounded more like a moan.

Kipling didn't seem to notice she'd lost the ability to

make coherent words. He was too busy exploring the skin of her breasts and learning how she tasted.

He'd made a joke once about being both a sex god and her every fantasy come to life. Under him, on his bed, with his lips and hands and mouth and tongue doing things that no other lover ever had and making her body experience sensations she hadn't known were possible, she agreed with him.

She eventually managed to work her body in such a way that he was under her. She ran her hands over his chest, loving the feel of him beneath her fingertips, but irritated his shirt was still partially on.

"This is why I wanted you completely naked," she said, fumbling with the buttons and coming to the conclusion that coordination and arousal didn't mix.

"Rip it off," he said through clenched teeth.

"What?"

"I want to see you rip it off me." Even in the darkness, the moon gave enough light for her to see his eyes blazing with desire. "Now, Alyssa. Show me how much you want me. Be wild for once. Be wild for me."

That was all he had to say and the only motivation she needed. She took the rejection she'd feared, the uncertainty she'd experienced, and meshed them together with the desire she could no longer deny, the need she felt, and the compulsion to do as he requested because she *was* wild for him. She wanted the world to know, but she'd start with him.

She tightened her hold, took a deep breath, and with a yell and a pull, the shirt came off. She held it airborne just long enough for him to see before dropping it off the side of the bed.

"Damn, Alyssa," he said. "I think that was the hottest thing I've ever seen in my life."

"You haven't seen anything yet," she promised, not waiting for him to reply but taking his boxer briefs and pulling them down in one smooth motion. Before he could speak, she engulfed his length in her mouth.

Though she didn't doubt her ability to give a decent blowjob, she was pleased Kipling seemed to be enjoying it, as evidenced by the way his hands fisted the sheets at his side. She would have preferred his hands to be in her hair, but she told herself she couldn't have everything.

"Alyssa, are you okay?" he asked.

Kipling was much more astute than she gave him credit for, however. He must have sensed her hesitation or picked up on some other movement she didn't recall making.

After what had transpired between them earlier, she wasn't about to lie to him now. "I like having my hair pulled, and I saw you holding the sheets. I thought, if you wanted to..."

"I do, but I didn't want to presume you would."

He didn't have to say anything more. She went back to what she'd been doing moments before, and it wasn't too long until his hands found their way to the exact place she wanted them. She hummed her pleasure around him as he tightened his fists and pulled.

"Yeah," he said, his voice laced with pleasure. "I knew you'd like it dirty. Such a dirty girl for me, aren't you?"

She didn't know how he expected her to answer with him in her mouth, but he kept on whispering, most of it so low she couldn't make it out.

It didn't take long until his breathing became choppy and the muscles in his stomach tightened. His hands became more urgent as he tried to pull her away.

"Alyssa, please. Not like this. I want to be inside you."

It was his "please," combined with the hair pulling, that made her stop. "I'd have been perfectly happy to continue, you know," she told him. "For future reference."

"Future reference?" he questioned, flipping her to her back and coming up and over her body so he was level with her eyes. "I'll keep that in mind. Right now, I have more pressing matters to attend to."

"You do?" she asked. "What would those be?"

"Well," he said, clearly getting into his playful nature, which she loved. "I'm going to start here"—he nibbled on her neck—"and work my way here"—he brushed her torso —"before ending somewhere along here." He stroked her thigh.

As soon as he touched her thigh, she froze.

"What?" he asked, obviously picking up on her change in demeanor.

"Please, please, please tell me you have a condom."

"Alyssa." He propped himself up on his elbow and looked down on her while drawing figure eights along her belly. "I've wanted you for months. Do you think there is even the slightest chance of me not being prepared?"

She wanted to tell him he didn't actually answer the question, but before she could get the words out, he spoke first.

"I not only have *a* condom, I have an entire box."

"Pretty sure of yourself, Mr. Benedict?" She raised an eyebrow, just because he'd brought it up earlier.

"No, Officer Adams," he replied with a grin. "Just an eternal optimist."

She laughed, loving how he joked along with her. Then he brought his lips down on hers, and within seconds, she wasn't able to focus on anything other than his touch and what it made her feel.

He wasn't a gentle lover, and for that she was grateful. She appreciated a man who wasn't afraid to touch her. One who didn't act as though she were made of glass.

She didn't have to worry about any of that with Kipling. His hands were knowledgeable, and he somehow knew how and where to touch to drive her wild. Most of the men she'd been with before had rushed through foreplay, but not Kipling. He took his time. In his arms, she felt like a newly discovered masterpiece. Not only because he was so thorough, but because he seemed so full of joy, for lack of a better word, to be the one doing the exploring.

After, when every other man she'd been with would roll over and sleep, once he disposed of the condom, he took her in his arms, pulled her to his chest, and told her how beautiful she was while drawing who knows what across her back.

He made her feel incredible, and while she'd always enjoyed sex, it seemed *more* with Kipling.

By the time her eyelids started to grow heavy, she knew she was in major trouble. Kipling had effectively stolen a bit of her heart, and she knew it'd always stay with him.

Chapter Fourteen

The next morning, Alyssa expected there to be tension between her and Kipling and was surprised when he casually kissed her good morning. They were still in bed and enjoying being lazy for a few minutes.

He stroked her back. "Do you still think today's a good day to visit your parents?"

She snorted. "No day is a good day to see those two, but yes. Might as well do it today."

"Anything in particular I should know?" he asked.

She wondered how different things would be if she were meeting his parents for the first time and felt an unexpected jolt of sadness at the realization she would never have the chance.

She stretched against him. "To be honest, I haven't seen them in years, and the last time, things were tense." She felt bad admitting that to him. After all, she at least had one living parent. "How about I make us some coffee?"

"Only if you want," he said, but she was already halfway out of bed.

"I don't think we should tell them all the details," she

said. "That it's Jade and your connection with her. I think we leave everything high level."

He nodded. "That's completely your call. I'll go along with whatever you think is best. What time should we go?"

"I think sometime late this morning." She slipped a shirt on and didn't miss the pinkish-red blooms on her torso, a result of Kipling's lavish kisses and explorations the night before. Every time she looked at them, she remembered a new part of the night before and she smiled.

Kipling's eyes grew wide as he took in the marks on her body. "Alyssa," he said, his voice heavy with emotion. "I'm so sorry. I didn't mean to be so rough."

She held up her hand. "Don't you dare apologize for anything that happened last night. If I didn't like you rough, I would have told you last night. Understand?"

"Yes, ma'am," he said, and he actually smiled.

"Now, I was thinking we head to my parents' house around eleven and not call beforehand. I believe the element of surprise will work in our favor." At his questioning glance, she added, "I'm not saying they'll lie, but something doesn't feel right about them whenever they talk about my sister. I don't want to give them time to think."

"Again, it's your call. You know them best."

She actually didn't feel like she knew them at all.

His eyes danced with the mischief she'd noted the night before. "My last question is what on earth are we going to do for the next two hours until it's time to leave?"

She'd just put her shirt on, but though it felt foolish, she walked over to him and drew it up and over her head. "I have an idea or two."

"Show me," he said, slipping his hands under her bra strap and arousing the same feeling he had the night before.

Except, this time, the feelings were even more intense because she knew exactly what was in store for her.

* * *

A FEW MINUTES BEFORE ELEVEN, Kipling parked his car in front of the house where Alyssa told him to stop. They sat for several seconds, neither one of them saying anything.

"The lights are on," he finally said.

She nodded.

He looked at the house and tried imagining what it had been like growing up inside. How it felt knowing her sister had been murdered, and not being allowed to speak her name. How hard it must have been for someone who loved her sister.

What did it say about her mother, that she let her husband dictate such a thing? How could she allow him to demand she never speak of her own child? There were no words of encouragement he could give to make Alyssa feel better. All he could do was place his hand on her knee and give it a gentle squeeze. *I'm here if you need me.*

Alyssa looked up, and he knew that was what she'd needed. "Thank you," she whispered softly.

Not only were the lights on in the house, but there was a car parked in the driveway. He wasn't sure how many cars her parents had, but the evidence pointed toward someone being at home.

They walked to the front door with him one step behind her. This was her family, and she would be the one to make the first move.

Seconds after Alyssa rang their doorbell, the curtains in the front room moved. Before too long, an older version of Alyssa stood in the doorway, looking at them.

"Good Lord," was all she said, her face a deathly chalky white as if she'd seen a ghost.

"Who's at the door, Mildred?" could be heard from inside.

It didn't appear Mildred was going to answer him. She stood there in shock, looking at both her daughter and Kipling.

"Mildred?" came the voice again.

When she still didn't answer, they heard footsteps approach. From where he stood, Kipling watched a giant of a man appear. He was huge, with muscles that could probably snap Kipling in half like a twig. The giant looked at him with a snarl, then at Alyssa, and then back to him.

Kipling was used to working with his share of giants, both in and out of the boardroom, and he wasn't about to let this man intimidate him. A quick glance at Alyssa made it clear she wasn't going to back down either.

She took a step forward, but the man held out his hand to stop her. "Hell no," he said. "Not again. Get off my property and out of my sight. Don't ever come back."

Beside him, Alyssa's mother wailed, "No!"

"Mildred," he said. "Can't you see the same thing is happening? The exact same thing. I won't have it. They need to leave."

Finally, Alyssa spoke up. "What do you mean, 'the exact same thing'?"

"Go away," her stepfather said and slammed the door in front of them.

"Asshole," Alyssa mumbled under her breath.

Kipling took a step back from the closed door. "Well," he said. "That was certainly interesting."

Alyssa rubbed the back of her neck, and Kipling swallowed the remarks he wanted to say. He would bite his tongue for now.

Alyssa banged on the door. "It doesn't work that way. We're not going anywhere."

There was only silence on the other side of the door.

She lowered her voice. "If I knew the neighbors wouldn't call the police, I'd shoot the damn door off its hinges."

"As much as I'd like to see that," Kipling admitted, "I agree. Not the best course of action here."

"Mom." Alyssa knocked on the door. "Mom, please. You know I wouldn't be here if it wasn't important. I'm close to solving this case. Help me."

They looked at each other when the sound of raised voices came from inside the house. The sound escalated until it suddenly stopped. The door creaked open only a little, but wide enough for them to see the red eyes and wet cheeks of Alyssa's mother.

"Mom." Alyssa pushed the door open further and wrapped her arms around her mom. The older woman sobbed, and Kipling heard the low murmurs of mother and daughter talking as they walked farther into the house. He took a step forward to join them.

Alyssa's stepdad blocked him. "You're not welcome in my house."

Kipling took a step backward, wanting the man to understand the truth of his next words. "Listen to me," Kipling said. "Someone has threatened Alyssa's life, and I take that sort of thing very seriously. I don't care what you have against her. I don't care what you have against me. Neither of those matters as long as that threat exists. And for as long as it does, I'm going to be right by her side to make sure she's not harmed. I don't care if you like it. I don't care if you agree with it. This has nothing to do with you. It has nothing to do with your murdered stepdaughter. It has everything to do with keeping *Alyssa* safe. Do you understand?"

Everything fell strangely silent when he finished speaking. He no longer heard Alyssa and her mother talking. Without saying a word, her stepfather moved to the side, allowing him to pass, and Kipling walked into the hallway where the women stood.

"Mrs. Adams," he said, holding his hand out to her. "Kipling Benedict. Nice to meet you."

The poor woman didn't seem to know whether to talk to him or not. She looked from him to her husband to her daughter and back again to Kipling. Mildred shook his hand but didn't reciprocate his sentiment. She sighed. "What can we do for you? I'm assuming you didn't come by to see how we are doing."

Alyssa hadn't been lying when she'd said tension remained between her and her parents.

Not only that, but her mother once more looked cold and distant. Her expression was flat when she spoke after no one answered her question. "I suggest we all go sit down."

Kipling turned around to head in the direction Mrs. Adams indicated and almost ran into the Neanderthal, now holding a newspaper.

"There." He shoved the paper at Alyssa. "Look at that, look at the two of you, and tell me what you think."

At first, Kipling thought he was looking at a picture of himself, but as he kept looking, it became obvious it was his father, though he looked different from the man in his memory. Kipling couldn't remember his father being as happy or smiling as brightly as the photo showed. And the woman at his side was not his wife of almost twenty years. Rather, it was woman who looked all too much like Alyssa.

She must have noticed the same thing at the same time, because she gasped.

"Striking resemblance, isn't there?" her stepfather asked, but he didn't wait for an answer. "I thought so too. So if you think you're going to sit here in my house, like your sister and his sorry excuse for a father, you can think again."

"It's not like that," Alyssa said quietly.

Kipling wanted to touch her, to place his hand on the lower part of her back, to give her some sort of strength, some sort of secret sign to let her know he was with her. But his actions would not go unnoticed by her stepfather, and that wouldn't end well for anyone.

Alyssa pushed past her stepfather to continue into the other room. They all followed her, first Kipling, then her mother, and her stepfather trailing behind. Kipling had a chance to take the briefest glance around the room. For all intents and purposes, it was a typical middle-class house in a typical middle-class neighborhood.

"What was that I overheard you say about Alyssa being threatened?" Alyssa's mother asked once they'd all sat down.

"There's been some recent activity in the case. New evidence has been brought to light," Alyssa said. "Whoever killed my sister..." She looked at her stepfather briefly, letting him know she wouldn't say her name. "We believe he's still alive and might be after me."

"How is he involved?" her stepfather asked with a nod toward Kipling.

Kipling raised his eyebrow at Alyssa. *Do we tell him?*

She shook her head.

Kipling cleared his throat. "I have a family member we

fear has been kidnapped. Based on some of the similarities, we think she may have been taken by the same man. We need to find her and put whoever is behind this away for good. We don't want her—or anyone else, for that matter—to meet the same end your stepdaughter did."

Certainly, her stepfather would understand and agree. Of course he wouldn't want anybody to meet the same fate as his stepdaughter. But as it turned out, her stepfather wasn't like normal people.

"She deserved what she got," he said. "Being a whore for your father."

Kipling closed his eyes. If he stood any chance of swallowing the rage building up inside him and not unleashing it on Mr. Adams, he needed to keep his eyes off the man for a few seconds. A couple of deep breaths, and he felt calm enough to continue.

"Sir," Kipling said, far more evenly than he felt, "your stepdaughter was killed in a vicious and violent attack. Nobody, I repeat, *nobody*, no matter what they have done, deserves to have their life end that way."

Mr. Adams didn't say anything but leaned back into his chair and crossed his arms. The look he gave Kipling was one of pure hatred.

Mrs. Adams, on the other hand, acted visibly distressed. She looked at both of them, seeming to ignore her husband on purpose. "What can we do? Do you need to see something?"

"What we'd really like is to see her room," Alyssa told her mother. "Along with the items the police gave you."

"Of course," her mother said. "Everything is still in there." She took a side-glance at her husband. He didn't seem any happier. "I believe your stepfather and I will go out for lunch. We'll leave the key here in case you finish and need to go before we get back. Just lock up and put the key under the mat." The understanding and unsaid meaning, of course, was that he and Alyssa would be long gone when they returned.

"How long do you think you'll be out?" Kipling asked.

"Probably about three hours," Mildred said. "We have some shopping to do as well."

Mr. Adams looked less than thrilled to be shopping or going out, much less leaving Alyssa and a Benedict in his house alone. But he stood and followed his wife out the door.

Kipling didn't think it was in his imagination he could hear the man yell as he walked with his wife to their car.

Chapter Fifteen

Alyssa watched her parents drive away with a mixture of anger, shock, and embarrassment. She couldn't believe their actions toward Kipling.

"I'm so sorry," she said. "I had no idea they would be so rude."

Kipling shook his head. "There's no need to apologize for them not liking me. There are plenty of people who feel the same. At least your parents have a reason."

"But you didn't do anything to them," she said.

"No, not me personally," he said. "But my dad."

"It's not right. You shouldn't be judged on what your parents did," she said.

"Unfortunately, a lot of us are. And in this case, it's clear why your parents aren't happy to see me."

His words sounded sincere, but as they walked into the hallway, she wondered if he was being truthful or if her parents' actions upset him more than he let on.

"Which room is hers?" he asked.

Preparing herself for what she would find, Alyssa straightened her shoulders and led him into her sister's room. She stopped in the doorway, blinking back tears. She always felt her sister's presence so heavily in this room.

"It's okay." He stopped behind her and placed his hands on her shoulders. "I'm right here with you."

His touch did more than anything she could have done on her own, and she stepped farther into the room. As expected, her mother still hadn't changed anything since her sister's death. Everything was exactly the way it had been the day she walked out. She bet her stepfather hated that.

It had been years since Alyssa had been in the room. The last time she'd stood there, she still felt her sister. But that was no longer the case, and her sister's memory seemed faded as well. Alyssa wasn't sure if that was good or bad, finally deciding not to think about it because, no matter what the answer ended up being, she'd cry.

She needed to remove her personal bias. To be the policewoman she'd claimed to be when Kipling first asked her if she was too personally involved.

He stood off to the side, watching her, but not with doubts in his eyes.

"I can do this," she told him.

"I know you can."

She held out her hand. "Let me see the crime-scene photo."

He took the picture out of the folder he carried and handed it to her.

Though she had verified the night before that the purse wasn't in the photo, she wanted to check one more time to make sure she wasn't overlooking anything.

Not seeing anything in the photo, she looked at Kipling. "Ready to look in the box?"

He nodded solemnly. "Need me to get it? Is it in here?"

"Top shelf in the closet."

She watched as he went to retrieve the box and wondered how he would have reacted if one of his brothers had been kidnapped or killed.

But one of his own *had* been kidnapped, most likely by the same man who'd killed her sister.

"We're going to get him," she said when he returned with the box. "I'm sorry. I make such stupid promises sometimes."

"In that case, put me down as stupid right along with you, because I believe we're going to get him too."

Kipling glanced around, obviously trying to find a place to put the box. The only piece of furniture with any free space was the bed. He walked instead to the middle of the room and sat on the rug. Alyssa joined him.

"Do you want open it?" he asked.

"No, you go ahead." Truth be told, she had always been the one to open the box. She wanted to see if watching someone else do it would reveal anything new.

Kipling took the lid off and looked at her. "I know it's okay to touch the stuff inside, but I still feel like I shouldn't."

She nodded, knowing exactly how he felt, and watched as he took the items out of the box one at a time. There wasn't much, and by far the largest item was the purse.

She reached for it, but he said, "Wait."

"What?"

"Where is the Finition Noire envelope?" He shuffled through the remaining items in the box. "I don't see it here."

"I took it with me the last time." She shrugged. "Call me crazy, but I could see it getting lost or stolen."

"Makes sense."

"I mean, it's all already been looked over. It's not like I was stealing evidence or anything."

"Alyssa," he said, "you don't have to explain yourself to me. You're the expert here. I'm not going to question you." He held the purse up. "I'll let you do the honors."

"Humor me," she said. "Look it over and see if you can find the hidden compartment."

He gave her a look that told her he didn't think he'd have any trouble at all. It was a basic clutch with a small strap, and while most of the girls in her troop had opted to put the hidden pocket along the inner lining, she thought it was hidden better by putting it in the folder flap. While she knew the person who had killed her sister had more than likely found the compartment, she wanted to see if she could fool Kipling.

She watched him look over and through the purse. It was so hard to believe he was the same man who drove her up a wall after they first met. How wrong she'd been about him then. At the time, she thought he was a spoiled playboy who only cared about money and women. She couldn't have been more wrong.

She'd seen up close how fiercely protective of his family he was. Before she'd arrested him, she'd looked into his business dealings and discovered a man who was tough but fair. Even those who opposed him at the negotiation table spoke highly of him.

The papers loved to paint him as an egotistical philanderer, but he'd rather spend his evenings at home. In the entire time she'd known him, she'd never seen or heard of him taking a woman out to dinner, much less participating in anything anywhere near debauchery.

Kipling looked up from the purse. "Okay, I admit it. You've stumped me. Where is it?"

She was surprised he hadn't located it, and for the first

time, she held out real hope that maybe whatever Allison had put in the purse, if anything, remained.

She took the purse and shifted it in her hands, flipped it over, and exposed the hidden seam.

Kipling smiled. "I'm impressed."

"Thank you, but what will truly be impressive is if we find anything inside."

"Open it."

She didn't have to be told twice. Within seconds she had the compartment open. She took a deep breath and glanced at Kipling. He gave her a big smile of encouragement. Reaching into the space a little larger than a business-sized envelope, she honestly didn't expect to feel anything, but she froze when her fingers brushed paper.

"Alyssa?" Kipling asked.

"I feel something."

He looked as shocked as she felt. "What is it? Take it out."

Silently, she grabbed the papers and pulled them out. Someone, her sister, she suspected, had bound them together with a rubber band.

"Oh my goodness," she said. "It's more than a sheet or two."

Excitement bubbled up in her stomach, but as she unfolded the documents, she felt something else. It was hope, and she hadn't experienced hope in a long time.

Looking through the stack of papers, a handwritten note stood out. Seeing her sister's handwriting for the first time after so many years brought tears to her eyes.

"The note first?" she asked Kipling.

"Whatever you want," he said.

Obviously, he knew what a toll it took on her to see her

sister's handwriting. "I feel like we're getting somewhere, finally," she said.

"I agree."

She picked up the note and read out loud, "I don't know who's reading this. But I kind of hope it's Alyssa. Whoever you are, I'm probably dead. I have only one thing to ask. Please, if it is at all possible, please don't let him get Jade. She is all that is good and right with the world, and he will destroy her. Please, please, please keep her away from him.

"But I'm getting ahead of myself. I've always heard to start at the beginning, and while that's good advice, I'm not really sure where the beginning is. I'll start with why I came back.

"For one, I thought Franklin might be interested in seeing his daughter. Apparently, he was not. He wouldn't see me, much less Jade. I don't know why I was surprised. I told him when I called that I knew I should have gone by his house first. He got very angry and said he didn't want to see me or his daughter again. And then, because I'm a glutton for punishment, I went home. They wouldn't let me see Alyssa, and then I was told neither I nor my child was welcome. That's how I ended up at this homeless shelter. It wasn't my first choice, but I have a five-year-old and she needs to eat and have a bed to sleep in.

"So here I was, feeling all sorry for myself, and he showed up. I called him my Miracle Man. I was too blind to see the truth then, but he only had eyes for Jade. The first time he came by, he said his name was Howard and he was friends with Franklin. He leaned close, like he was going to tell me a secret, and whispered how his friend had always wanted a daughter. Then he said he'd let me stay at his house while we planned how to approach Franklin.

"I knew something was off as soon as we moved in. It

wasn't a typical house. I mean, it was a house, right in the historic district and everything. I guess what I mean is, it wasn't like a home. There were all these strange men walking in and out at all hours. I asked him about it once, and he just said they were business associates. I think he knew I didn't believe him.

"There were long stretches when he was gone, and one day when he was out and no one else was around, I decided to snoop. That's when I learned the truth. He also goes by the name King, and he is mean and evil and vicious. I should have known something wasn't right the way he kept brushing me off whenever I brought up Franklin. It wasn't until he'd told me to shut the fuck up about Franklin that I knew he would never approach him and I decided to snoop.

"Now I wish I didn't. I feel sick thinking about the things he's done and what he's planning to do. I took what I dared, to have something as proof if I ever got away, although that's looking less and less likely. I think his office has cameras and, if that's the case, he knows that I know everything about him. For the moment, Jade and I are back at the shelter, but I know we can't stay. We're leaving tonight.

"These papers are confirmation of the plans he has for killing Franklin. He's going to make it look like an airplane accident. He's still working out the how and when details, but trust me, the enclosed docs have what you need if you look hard enough. One is an email from Howard confirming Franklin's travel plans. Another is Howard sending that confirmation to an unknown third party, telling them the plan to take out Franklin was good to move forward.

"The other thing you should know about him is that he is running several businesses. But not the kind you're thinking of. They are storefronts for people to shop for women. I don't think I need to expand on that.

"That's all," Alyssa whispered. She blinked the tears out of her eyes and tried not to think about how she'd failed both her sister and her niece.

She wasn't sure what she had expected to find when she looked his way, but it most certainly was not the look of absolute horror she found. "Kipling?"

"Howard." He spoke the name through clenched teeth.

"What?" she asked, too caught up in memories of her sister to make sense of what he'd said.

"Howard Germain. He has to be the person appointed as Jade's guardian." He ran his fingers through his hair. "I can't believe I didn't see it until now. Especially after we discussed how odd it was that his daughter, Elise, knew we had a sister."

One by one, several pieces of the puzzle making up the case fell into place in Alyssa's mind, yet with each seemingly answered question, two more popped up in its place. And how much more must Kipling be feeling the same thing? Howard Germain was a longtime friend of the Benedict family.

God, what a mess.

"Why didn't your parents get custody of Jade?" Kipling asked. "They should have, right? Why didn't they?"

Alyssa shook her head. "I don't know. They've never mentioned a granddaughter." Her stomach twisted at the thought that her mom had rejected her own flesh and blood. She jumped up.

"What?" Kipling asked.

"There has to be paperwork somewhere, right? I'm going to rip this place apart until I find it."

He didn't say anything, but followed her.

Alyssa thought there were three possible places the paperwork might be: a safety deposit box, her mother's bedside table, or the safe they kept their important papers in. She opted to try the safe first since it was closer and she didn't want to go into her mother's bedroom if she didn't have to.

She found what she was looking for at the bottom of the safe, buried under a handful of two-dollar bills.

"Oh my god." She passed the court documents to Kipling. "Part of me hoped they had nothing to do with it, but they did. They *gave* her to him."

"Bastard didn't even give her his name." Kipling read through the pages quickly. "Kaja Jade German. What an ass."

"No wonder she feels like she doesn't belong anywhere." Overwhelming sadness washed over Alyssa.

Beside her, Kipling reached for his phone, his expression showing he felt the same. "I'm going to fix this." He put the phone on speaker and made a call. "No matter what."

She only hoped it wasn't too late.

"Knox," Kipling said into the phone. "Howard Germain."

He didn't need to explain. She heard the middle Benedict brother's curses through the phone.

Kipling glanced over at Alyssa. "We're at Alyssa's parents' house. We just found papers naming him as guardian and a lot more." He shuffled through the pages. "We also have information her sister obtained that appears to prove he was behind the airplane accident, as well as human-trafficking allegations. I'm not sure any of it would hold up in court. We won't know exactly what we have until we can get somewhere to look at it properly."

From the other end of the phone came a low whistle. "I can't believe he's into all that," said Knox.

"We can't, either. It's like the man we thought we knew never existed."

"There's something else," Knox said.

"More than what we've already learned?" Kipling asked. "I don't know if I can process much more."

"This is important. You two have been staying at the beach place?"

"Yes."

"I was getting ready to call you. Germain has bought the property on both sides."

Alyssa was positive her expression mirrored Kipling's. He had been so certain no one knew the place existed.

"How long has he owned them?" Kipling asked.

"It's hard to tell with any certainty." From the sound of it, Knox was typing. "From the online records, they appear to have switched hands a few times, but I can't determine if these are real businesses or just more fabrications like Finition Noire. If we assume they are fake, he's owned the land for over ten years. If it's just been since he's listed, maybe a handful."

"Either way, it's not good," Kipling said.

"I don't think you two should go back there," Knox said.

"I agree, but we're not returning to Benedict House, either. I'm fairly certain he's after me and Alyssa now, so I'd like to keep the focus off you guys. Benedict House is the best place for all of you, but don't go out if you don't have to. Make sure Keaton and Tilly are adequately protected, and don't let Bea out of your sight."

"Never doubt it."

"I'll call in and keep you updated when I can."

The brothers hung up after saying goodbye.

Alyssa couldn't help looking over at Kipling. "I have no idea what to do next or where to go."

He shook his head. "I don't either."

* * *

KIPLING HAD NEVER FELT MORE worthless. If he were alone, he'd be okay. Well, maybe not okay, but at least he could handle it better. He stood up and walked to the window. It wasn't only him, not by any stretch. He had Alyssa with him. Both of his younger brothers and Tilly and Bea were at his house, but he wasn't there to ensure their safety. Most of all, there was Jade. Who knew where she was.

He felt like a complete failure.

Out the window and over the expanse of the neighborhood, people walked around, living their normal lives, looking as if nothing out of the ordinary was happening. And for them, it probably wasn't. He'd never wanted to switch places with someone so badly before in his entire life.

Alyssa came up behind him and placed her hands on his shoulders. He leaned back toward her, and she wrapped her arms around him.

"I would say it'll be okay," she whispered, "but I don't know that it will. But I do know that we're in it together."

He took her hand. "That means a lot more than you think it does. Thank you."

"I don't think we should stay here," she said.

"You're right," he said. "I don't want to put your parents in any danger."

"I guess we can't go to Benedict House either."

"Correct."

"How do you think he found out about the beach place?"

"I'm not sure," he said. "It's possible Mom told him. I know they were all at the same college. I'm not sure how close Mom was to Howard, though." He sighed deeply. "Anywhere we are, we'll put people in danger. The other option is to sleep in my car." He raised an eyebrow at her. "How are you at camping?"

"Horrible," she said. "If I were still with the force, we could ask for a safe house. On second thought, forget I said that. I doubt those would be safe either. Who knows if the police department is in on this with him."

"Let's look at this a different way. What are our objectives?"

"Get Jade back."

"Yes," he said. "In order to do that, we have to know where she's being kept. Unfortunately, whoever is keeping her—Howard Germain, I assume—hasn't contacted me lately. Knox is trying to track him down but isn't having any luck so far."

"The other thing we need to do," she said, "is to bring him down, but we don't have information to do that yet, either."

"Right."

"So what do you think we should do?"

"If you think you're up to it, I propose we go to the homeless shelter. The one where your sister stayed. Make it out to be an unannounced visit of Benedict Industries. We'll do a little bit of snooping and see what we can find."

"Let's go."

King

Thirty-five years ago
Harvard University

As far as parties went, Howard Germain rated this one a solid four out of ten. With little chance of redemption, based on a glance at his watch. Kappa Sigma had one planned tomorrow night. Maybe it would be better. He headed to the door, ready to leave.

"Howard."

He turned to his best friend and roommate, Franklin Benedict. It was highly unlikely Frank wanted to walk back to their apartment together, since he'd broken up with his latest piece of fluff. No, if he knew Frank, he'd be looking for a new bed bunny to enjoy for an hour or two. Odds were, the bastard would find one.

"Benedict." Howard kept his voice flat. "What are you still doing vertical?"

Frank laughed as if it was the funniest joke he'd ever heard. "I found her, man."

"Then why are you standing here instead of screwing her brains out?"

"Not a cock toy for the night. *Her*. The future Mrs. Benedict."

Howard played along. He'd been introduced to numerous future Mrs. Benedicts for as long as he could remember. Hell, there had been two in the past month. This latest one would be no different. But, to humor the guy and so he could leave sooner, he looked to his right, where Frank pointed.

Howard didn't say anything for several seconds. He wasn't sure he took a breath.

The woman in question was stunning, and even that was an understatement. It was more than her looks, though she was certainly beautiful. It was her entire being. The way she stood, the way she smiled; hell, even the way she tilted her head to the left as she talked to the women around her.

He could see why she'd caught Frank's eye. His roommate preferred blondes, and this woman's color looked completely natural. Nothing like the out-of-the-bottle jobs so many women had.

"Come on," Frank said. "Let's go introduce ourselves. I see Lisa just walked up to her."

Lisa was a women Frank had dated for six hours and left.

"You sure you want to go up to her while Lisa's up there? Aren't you afraid she'll tell your future wife what an ass you are?"

"Lisa and I parted on good terms."

"I'm not sure your definition of 'good terms' meshes so well with the rest of the world's."

Frank punched him on the arm, but Howard wasn't joking.

The crowd wasn't as heavy as it'd been just an hour ago. Apparently, Howard wasn't the only one who thought the current party lacked something vital. But the small crowd meant it took them less time to make their way to where the girls were.

"Ladies," Frank said as they approached the small group.

As it turned out, Frank did walk home with Howard that night and even slept alone. But he had a dinner date for the next weekend with Helen (or the future Mrs. Benedict, as he kept calling her), and he talked about nothing else as they made their way home.

"What do you think?" he asked Howard at one point in the conversation.

Howard knew Frank didn't care one way or the other about what he thought of his newest love interest. Likewise, Howard didn't feel like discussing his thoughts about Helen with the guy he knew would toss her to the side once he got his dick inside her.

So instead of agreeing with Frank that, yes, she was gorgeous and, no, he'd never seen bluer eyes on anyone, he answered truthfully.

"I think I hate you."

Chapter Sixteen

"We have a problem," Alyssa said about five minutes after leaving her parents' house for the shelter.

Kipling glanced at her. She stared at the passenger-side mirror, watching something on the highway behind them. Every so often, she glanced at the rearview mirror.

"What do you see?" he asked.

"We're being followed."

His heart started to pound, and he gripped the steering wheel tighter. His gaze flickered to the rearview mirror. He didn't see anything, but that didn't mean it wasn't there.

"Black SUV," she said. "They're a couple cars behind us at the moment, but I know they're there." She was very calm, and even though he reminded himself she did this for a living, he didn't see how it was possible for her to be so calm.

"Have any suggestions as to what we should do?"

"Turn right up ahead at the next light," she told him. "Then take the immediate left."

He followed her directions. "Still there?"

"Yes." She glanced over her shoulder. "But I didn't expect to shake them that quickly. Make a U-turn at that hotel on your left. This is where we lose them."

He made a quick U-turn at the spot she indicated and couldn't help smiling as her plan became clear. As soon as they made the turn, the light changed, and hoards of tourists swarmed the street, making it impossible for anyone to follow. Kipling forced himself not to look at the black SUV as they drove past.

"What now?" he asked when the crowd thinned and there was no longer anyone behind them.

"We ditch your car."

"I was afraid you were going to say something like that. You know that means we ditch our hotel room for the night."

"You didn't seriously plan for us to sleep in your car, did you?"

"No, but it was nice to have options."

"We need to leave it somewhere crowded."

"I have an idea," he said. "What about the cruise terminal? I think there are ships coming in today. It'll be very crowded and congested, with a good number of police officers around."

"Perfect."

They were already near the waterfront, so it only took a few minutes for them to arrive at the seaport. There should be a number of transportation options to pick from nearby.

"We should get on a bus," Kipling said without hesitation once they left his car at a large parking deck near the terminal. "We can blend in with the crowd better. And it's probably the last thing anyone would expect us to do."

Alyssa bit her bottom lip. "Sounds reasonable." She

stepped out of the stairway and into a crowd of people. "Come on," she called to him. "Hurry up."

Kipling wasn't sure how well they fit in with the crowd, as neither one of them looked like a tourist. But they made it to the bus station without anyone aiming a gun at them, so he took it as a win.

"Do we need to figure out where we're going?" he asked, standing next to Alyssa at a ticket kiosk.

"No, I'm getting us each a three-day pass. That way we can hop on the first bus we see and figure out where we're going once we're on. Right now, we need to get out of this part of the city."

Kipling had to agree. Nothing and no one looked suspicious or seemed to be paying them any mind. They waited with a large tourist group, hoping to blend in, and hopped on the first bus that appeared.

Kipling wove through the people standing, keeping a tight grip on Alyssa's hand. He half expected her to jerk away and tell him she was fine, but surprisingly enough, she didn't.

They found two empty seats and sat down. Alyssa immediately reached for her purse, and Kipling glanced around. Nothing seemed out of the ordinary, and he relaxed a bit. They appeared to be free for the moment.

The bus came to a stop, and they remained seated while people loaded and unloaded. Kipling tried to look at everyone who got on. No one looked their way. Another good sign.

Kipling glanced up when a skinny, relatively good-looking young man wearing baggy pants walked their way. The guy looked harmless.

Kipling's head hurt. He hated the bus, or he had the few

times he'd ridden one. He closed his eyes, hoping to ease the pounding in his head.

"Mama," a little boy behind him said in a hushed voice. "That man who got on has a gun."

Kipling's entire body tensed. It was probably nothing, but he wasn't going to chalk anything up to coincidence. He raised his eyelids a touch, enough so he could see but would still appear to be dozing.

The young man sat across the aisle from Alyssa, head nodding as he supposedly listened to music through earbuds. If he'd heard the boy, nothing in his body language gave it away. Kipling was fairly certain Alyssa had heard, but she gave nothing away, either. She hadn't tensed at all.

Trying to act casual, he rested his head on her shoulder, slipped a hand to her knee, and whispered, "Young man across from you has a gun. Not sure he's after us."

She kissed his cheek and murmured in his ear, "I heard. We should get off at the next stop."

"Let's go," he said, and they both stood and moved closer to the doors. Alyssa stayed at his side but turned her body to keep the gunman in her line of sight.

The bus slowly pulled to a stop, and when the doors opened, they sprinted outside. Neither one of them dared to look back, afraid of being too obvious.

"Over there." Alyssa pointed across the street to a shopping center. "Let's go to the second level. We can look down from there."

They sprinted across the street and up the flight of stairs. At the top, Kipling took a second to look down. Sure enough, the young man from the bus was crossing the street, talking on his phone.

"Shit," Kipling said.

* * *

As soon as her adrenaline dropped, Alyssa was going to crash, and it wasn't going to be pretty. The best she could hope for was to hold it together until they made it somewhere safe.

"There's a taxi over there," Kipling said, pointing just a short distance away. "I think we can make it there before he spots us."

Kipling continued to amaze her with his clear head and quick thinking. He never seemed to panic, but took everything in stride.

"Let's go," she said, and they sprinted toward the taxi.

"Where you going?" the driver asked when they slipped into the back seat.

She looked over her shoulder and shut the door. Thankfully, she didn't see anyone following.

"We should eat," Kipling said, sounding slightly out of breath. "It's been a long time since breakfast."

"That's fine." She wasn't hungry, but he was right. "I'm good with whatever you want."

While he gave the driver directions, she looked out the window. She spied the young guy reaching the top of the stairs as they pulled off. He never once looked their way.

Kipling had given the driver the name of a pizza joint on the other side of town, and she closed her eyes and told herself to relax while she had the chance. But it wasn't until Kipling put his arm around her and pulled her close that the tension left her body.

Much too soon, the taxi pulled up to the pizzeria, and she waited while Kipling paid the driver. When he finished, he turned to her and smiled. "Let's eat. I'm famished."

Typical male. Being followed by a stranger with a gun did nothing to curb his appetite. She was more tired than anything, and with the adrenaline coming down, the thought of food made her a touch queasy. But she needed to eat and knew she'd feel better with a full stomach.

"You go order," she told Kipling. "I'll grab a table outside by the window and be on the lookout."

"We're safe here," Kipling said. "At least for a while."

"Better to err on the side of caution."

She told him she didn't care what kind of pizza he got as long as he got her a big bottle of water. After a detour to the bathroom to freshen up and wash her hands, she took a seat at a table by the window.

Kipling was texting someone but placed their order a few minutes later and headed her way with two bottles of water.

"Just got a text from Knox," he said, sliding into the seat across from her. "I told him we'd call tonight and there were a few things we needed to talk to him about."

Alyssa nodded in between taking sips of water. "By things to talk about, you mean things you want him to hack into?"

"Yes," Kipling agreed. "I thought my way sounded a bit more legal."

She sighed. "I don't even care anymore."

"Hey." Kipling lifted a finger to raise her chin. "What's wrong?"

"Nothing," she said, but when he shook his head, she added, "I'm just tired, is all. It's been a crazy day. How can you be so calm?" It didn't mesh with her image of a shipping executive.

"Defense mechanism. I'm not thinking about it, therefore it doesn't exist." She must have looked perplexed, because he added, "It'll catch up with me later tonight and I'll crash."

She yawned. "I think it's already caught up with me."

Kipling stretched and leaned back in his seat, relaxing for the first time in hours. "Hopefully, we're in the clear now. We'll find somewhere safe, and then we'll both crash."

A waitress brought their pizza to the table, and Alyssa didn't miss the way she smiled at Kipling. For his part, Kipling pretty much ignored the woman.

After the waitress walked away, he reached for a slice. "Eat up."

She was on her second piece and Kipling on his fourth when she felt the familiar tickle on the back of her neck. Someone was watching. Her stomach turned and she put down the pizza slice in her hand. Her expression must have changed because Kipling's expression grew worried.

"What?" he asked.

"I'm not sure." She glanced around the immediate area. "Just a feeling."

"Shit."

"It may be nothing." She hoped that was the case.

"Unfortunately, it is something," he said, dread filling his voice. "Our young friend has returned. Behind you."

Her stomach felt queasy at thoughts of the man staring at them. "How close?" She slipped her hand to her purse, ready to pull out her weapon.

"Not very."

She allowed herself a deep breath. "Should we get up and escape through the café's back door?"

"Does the café have a back door?"

"I don't know. Surely it leads to an alley or something."

"Is that a chance we should take?"

"It'll be easier to give him the slip if we go through the back door instead of doing it in front of him." If there wasn't a back door, she could potentially be putting innocent people in danger. But if they stayed here, people outside the café would be in danger.

"Let's go." Kipling stood up, not moving toward the café until she got in front of him.

As she walked toward the entrance to the café, she pulled out an old badge and flashed it to the employees working inside. "Police. Is there a back entrance?"

The teenage boy working the register looked about ready to faint at her words, and the waitress standing next to him dropped a tray of drinks. Fortunately, she recovered quickly enough to nod and point toward the back.

Alyssa led the way, darting through the kitchen and out the back door. No sooner had the door closed behind them than they heard a commotion coming from inside the café.

Kipling cursed under his breath, looking around the alley surrounding them. "Damn it. It's a dead end."

Something inside the café crashed, and Alyssa jumped. "There's a pet store next door. Come on."

She ran the few steps to the back door of the pet store and prayed it wasn't locked. The sweetest sound in the world was a bell ringing as she opened the door. She flashed her badge again and, with Kipling behind her, ran out the main entrance and onto the street.

"This way," she said, dodging tourists and headed toward a church.

Kipling stayed at her side, and together they ducked under a construction barrier and into the lower level of the church. For several minutes, they stayed near the doorway, catching their breath and watching for anyone who may have followed.

Footsteps echoed behind them. Kipling spun around and Alyssa followed, gun drawn.

It was the young man from the bus, but he'd stopped walking and held his empty hands above his head. "Please," he said in an unexpected plea.

Alyssa didn't lower her weapon. "Why are you following us?"

"My name is Kevan. I need your help to rescue Jade," he said. "King's going to kill her."

"I don't believe you," Alyssa said. "Not about needing our help. I believe you're one of Howard Germain's minions, and you would say anything to get us to lower our guard."

"So you know who he is?" Kevan nodded. "That's good. At least I don't have to explain all of that to you. And you're right, I do work for him, and I'm risking my life reaching out to you like this. Please, you have to help me save Jade."

Alyssa wanted to believe him but couldn't allow herself to do so. "Why have you been following us?"

"You aren't the only ones being watched," Kevan said. "I had to play my part and look convincing. I'm the one who left the birth certificate in the oven."

Kipling nodded. "No one knows about the oven except family."

The oven was where Knox and Bea had found the birth certificate bearing Jade's name. Maybe Kevan was trying to help.

"King's been tracking you with your phones and Mr. Benedict's tablet," Kevan said.

"Fuck!" Kipling exclaimed.

"Leave them here and go to the school across the street.

There's a costume rack behind the stage in the auditorium. Disguise yourself. After that, go to the shelter by the docks. I'll meet you there after dark."

"What are you going to do?" Alyssa asked.

"Lead King on a wild goose chase and try not to get killed while doing so."

King

Thirty-four years ago
Thanksgiving

"Your mother told me things are getting pretty serious between Benedict and that girl he's been dating. You're going to be a senior next year. It's about time for you to think about settling down and getting married yourself. Any chance we'll be hearing something along those lines from you?"

Howard knew better than to curse at his father, so he bit back the string of words he wanted to say and instead replied with, "I'll make sure you're one of the first to know."

His dad thought his answer was funny for some reason and chuckled. Fortunately, after that, he patted Howard on the back and left him alone.

Damn it all. Like it wasn't enough Frank and Helen were the talk of the entire fucking campus, but now he had to hear about it from his own parents over Thanksgiving break? With Franklin having found an acceptable woman to marry, Howard would never hear the end of it about it being his time to do the same.

Unfortunately, he couldn't tell his father the truth. Couldn't tell him he had found the girl he wanted to marry. Or about how beautiful, smart, and perfect she was. Couldn't tell him, because she was well on her way to marrying his best friend.

It didn't make sense to anyone, least of all Howard. Frank's longest relationship before Helen had lasted two weeks, and that had been freshman year. Frank should have split up with Helen months ago, allowing Howard to swoop in and be the white knight. Then he could offer Helen a friendly face for support and, when she was ready, a man who would love her the way she deserved.

Unfortunately, Howard was seen only as Frank's roommate. Someone to take Helen's messages when she called and Frank wasn't there. Like a damn secretary.

Now that he thought about it, Frank had been out a lot lately. Obviously, they weren't together, since she was calling to speak with him.

Was Frank cheating on her?

Was it wrong Howard hoped he was?

The doorbell downstairs rang. Probably more cousins. Since he had no desire to see his cousins before he had to spend over an hour with them at the dinner table, he stayed in his room.

Curiously, though, instead of the noise downstairs dying out as one would expect, it grew louder and louder. He tried to remember which cousins were arriving today, but drew a blank. All he knew was listening to them was getting on his last nerve.

He paced in his room briefly, but doing so did nothing to help. Would they ever shut up?

Right as he was getting ready to stomp down to the main level and find out what the fuck had everyone in an uproar, his mother called.

"Howard!"

Damn it. He was going to have to see his cousins before dinner, after all.

"What?" he yelled back.

"Do come down. It's the most fabulous news."

Some of the talking faded, but before Howard could be thankful for the brief respite, an unexpected voice rang out above all the others.

Helen?

Helen was here. At his house. Why?

"Howard!" his mother called again.

He walked to the doorway of his room, still in awe that Helen was right downstairs, when he heard another voice.

Frank?

Why would the golden couple be at his house? He started down the stairs, but not with as much excitement as he'd felt before. Helen. Frank. Fabulous news.

He froze halfway and gripped the banister so tight he almost lost feeling in his fingers. He forced himself to breathe so he didn't fall headfirst down the stairs.

Oh, hell. No.

It couldn't be. Anything but that.

Because that would mean he was too late, and it couldn't be too late.

"Seriously, Howard," Frank said. "Get down here so I can ask you nice and proper to be my best man."

Too late.

Too late.

Chapter Seventeen

Kipling resisted the urge to tell Alyssa he wasn't completely sure they could trust Kevan. They'd had that argument three times in the hour and a half they'd been at the school. He doubted the fourth would produce a different result.

Though he had to admit, the young man had certainly been correct about the costume rack. He looked twenty years older with the clothes Alyssa had found. The shabby plaid shirt and oversize jeans hid his shape. Unfortunately, she couldn't find anything to mask his eyes. With a sigh, she finally handed him a pair of sunglasses. "Wear these."

He slipped them on, and she leaned back against the cluttered countertop. She studied him, rubbing her hand over her much-too-realistic-looking pregnant belly. He didn't know what she found that made it so convincing, and he honestly didn't care to know. All he could focus on at the moment was the way she looked pregnant and, even though he knew he shouldn't, he allowed himself to imagine for a second or two that it was real and it was his.

"Kipling?" she asked. "Are you ready to go?"

He glanced up from her fake baby belly. "What?"

She tilted her head. "I asked if you were ready to go."

"Yes." The glasses she'd found for him slipped down his nose. "Do I keep these on?"

"I'm afraid so."

He sighed and held out his hand. "If you were really the mother of my child, I'd drive. Or take a cab."

They walked to the shelter in silence. Kipling tried to keep his eyes on their surroundings. He couldn't stop feeling like, at any second, someone was going to jump out and say, "There they are," exposing them for all to see.

But nothing of the sort happened, and they arrived at the shelter with no issues.

"Let me do the talking," Alyssa said as they walked up to the front door.

Alyssa was all smiles when the woman turned their way and asked, "Can I help you?"

"I hope so," Alyssa said, drawing out her vowels and making her normally subtle Southern accent very intense. "I'm Lynda, and this is my husband, Lloyd. We're on our way to Savannah and need a place to spend the night. Normally, I wouldn't mind being on the streets, you know, but we did that last night, and I don't know if I can do that again." She rubbed her hands over her belly.

"Of course," the shelter worker smiled sweetly at Alyssa and then turned her attention to Kipling. "Would you mind taking the glasses off, Lloyd?"

Kipling looked at Alyssa. *Now what?*

Of course, Alyssa had anticipated the question and stood in between them. "He has to keep them on. He has this light sensitivity thing." She wrinkled her eyebrows. "Photo-something? I can't remember. All I know is this he can't take them off or he'll barf everywhere."

No more mention was made of his glasses, and instead, the worker flipped through a stack of papers. "Normally, we separate the men and women, but I don't think we'll do that in this case."

Alyssa and Kipling exchanged a *thank goodness* look.

"I have a private room I'm going to put you in since it's just for the night." She looked up with a grin. "Come with me, I'll show you around."

They followed her down a hallway. Kipling couldn't help but notice Alyssa looked more and more uneasy the more they walked.

"Men's bathroom is right there." The guide pointed with her left hand. "And the women's bathroom is right across the hall. Those are the closest to where you'll be staying."

They walked a few more steps and made it to an open door. "Here's your room. Everything you need should be in there, but come see me at the desk if it's not. Breakfast is at seven sharp." She didn't lead them inside, but bid them good night, turned, and went back to the desk.

Kipling put his hand on Alyssa's lower back as they walked inside. "Tell me what's wrong."

Alyssa took a deep breath and looked around the small room. It only contained a bed and two small chairs. "My sister was in a room like this. It never occurred to me to question why she had a private room."

Kipling didn't know how to respond, so he put his arms around her and held her close. "It's okay," he said, hoping it was the truth. "We're so close. We're going to find out what happened to your sister and get justice for her. We're going to find Jade, and the two of you are going to do all those aunt-and-niece things, like helping her get ready for a date and sharing ice cream when some jerk breaks up with her.

I'll see to it that you catch up and become the best of friends."

She chuckled. He felt the vibrations up and down his chest. "I know you can't promise any such thing, but it does make me feel better to hear you say them."

"If I could give up my entire fortune to ensure it happened, I'd do it in a second," he whispered in her ear.

As expected, moments before midnight, someone knocked on their door. Kipling opened it a crack.

Kevan spoke before Kipling could get a word out. "King knows you're here. He'll be here any second."

"How?" Alyssa asked.

"I don't know. All I know is that he's headed here, and when he makes it, you need to be somewhere else."

"Shit," Kipling said.

"You need to leave. Now." He looked over his shoulder again and lifted a hand in a half wave. When he turned back to them, his face was pale. "He's here. You can't leave through the door anymore." Another look over his shoulder. "Head out the window. Now!"

King

Thirty-three years ago
Wedding rehearsal dinner of Franklin and Helen

Everyone was calling it the wedding of the century. If it had been anyone else getting married, Howard would have laughed at how pretentious it sounded. The bride's family had spent a small fortune on the event, and damn near everyone was invited. And how the hell could anyone forget the ten bridesmaids? Ten. But the wedding of the century? Shouldn't that be reserved for royalty?

The real kind, that is. Not the kind that comes with a fake title given to you by the media to sell more papers.

But Howard couldn't focus on how ridiculous everything was. Everything was happening too fast, and he didn't know how to make it slow down. This time tomorrow, it would be too late. This time tomorrow, the only woman he'd ever loved would be married to his best friend.

Howard blamed himself for everything. After all, it wasn't as if the wedding had been a secret. They'd been planning the damn thing for almost two years. He had no room to say he didn't have time to do anything. The truth was, he'd been chicken. He'd been afraid.

It was obvious to him, and therefore should have been obvious to everyone, that Frank was seeing other women behind Helen's back. Howard would never forget the day he'd come home from class early only to find Frank in the kitchen, fucking a woman who wasn't Helen. He'd ignored the couple and went past them into his room, where he slammed the door. Until then, he'd only suspected Frank of cheating on his fiancée. It was so much worse to see it with his own eyes.

Even now, months later, he remembered feeling equal parts angry and bewildered.

Angry, because how could Frank cheat on Helen? Bewildered, because *why* would he cheat on Helen?

His first thought was to tell Helen. Further thinking convinced him it would be easier to show up and be the knight in shining armor, saving the day, as opposed to the bastard pointing out what an ass her fiancé was.

He risked a glance at Helen. She looked radiant, but was it all an act? Sitting at the head table, sharing whispers and kisses with Frank, she looked happy and in love.

Howard stood up and walked to the open bar to get a refill of his scotch.

It no longer mattered if she was pretending or blissfully in love. He was running out of time. The years had become months had become weeks had become days. Now, he was down to mere hours.

* * *

Hours later, Howard was on a mission. This was it. Now or never. His last chance.

He tried not to laugh at the thought that he had Frank to thank for the opportunity. If Frank had any idea what Howard planned to do, he'd never have asked his roommate to make sure his bride made it home safe. But he had, and Howard planned to grab it and take it for all it was worth.

Telling himself to settle down, he stepped outside.

His breath caught as it normally did when her beauty struck him. Although *beauty* seemed almost too common to describe her. Especially as she was currently, with moonlight bathing her.

"Helen?"

She turned to him and smiled. "Howard, how are you? I feel as if I haven't seen or spoken to you all day."

He shoved his hands in his pockets. "You have been a bit busy. It's understandable. After all, it's not like you get married every day."

She laughed, and as always when he heard that sound, his heart wanted to skip out of his chest. But tonight it was much more than skipping. Tonight, his heart jumped and raced because this night was so much more important than any other night.

He wondered if Helen saw anything different about him. Probably not. More than likely her head was going in fifteen thousand different directions. He was getting ready to make it fifteen thousand and one.

"Am I needed somewhere?" she asked, then frowned. "Surely not, it has to be after midnight. Do you have a watch?"

"It is after midnight. That's why I'm here. Frank asked me to make sure you got home safely." She still looked confused, so he explained, "It's your wedding day, so you can't see Frank until the big moment."

"Oh, right." She laughed again. "It is, isn't it? My

wedding day." She looped her arm through his. "And you're here to see me home. What a gentleman you are."

He bet *gentleman* would be the last word she'd call him after he told her what he was getting ready to do. Unfortunately, it couldn't be helped. He took a deep breath and said what he'd been trying to find the words to say for years.

"There's probably a better way to say this," he started. "But I'm out of time, and this is my only opportunity. Or more aptly, my last opportunity."

"Howard." She pulled back. "You're confusing me. What in the world?"

"Just listen to me, Helen."

She nodded. "Go on."

They were close enough to her apartment to walk. It being after midnight, there were very few other people out and about. A quick look around and he didn't see anyone else. Good. That meant no one to overhear.

"Frank is cheating on you." The words rushed out, and he felt so much lighter getting them off his chest. But a quick glance at Helen showed the burden now fell on her, and she found it too heavy to carry.

She stopped walking and, moving too fast for him to stop, slapped him harder than anyone ever had before. "How *dare* you!" She nearly spat the words at him. "And on my wedding day. I used to like you, Howard Germain. I thought you were a nice guy and a good friend to Frank. Now I see you're nothing but a miserable, sneaky snake. Go away. I'll make it home just fine."

"Helen." He'd known it wouldn't be easy. Had known she probably wouldn't believe him at first, but even knowing wasn't enough to take away the sting of being called a liar. "You have to believe me. I wouldn't be saying this if it wasn't true. You know me well enough to know I would never do anything to hurt you."

She stood a short distance away with her arms crossed, glaring at him like it was *his* fault her fiancé was a pig.

"I may have thought that before, but not now," she said. It was too dark to see if she'd found any of what he'd said to be truthful. All he could make out was the glare. "Even if what you said is true, you still waited until my wedding day to bring it up."

"That was wrong of me, but you have to believe me. I kept thinking you'd find out and I wouldn't have to be the one to tell you." Desperation raced through him; she didn't believe him, and he didn't know what to do to make her. Why hadn't he tried to tell her before now? An idea flashed through his mind. A foolhardy idea that would never work, but he knew he had to try. "Come with me."

"What?"

He held out his hand. "Come with me. Let's run away together. Just you and me. We won't tell anyone. I can love you like he can't." Something flashed in her eyes—*yes*, he was getting through! "There will never be anyone else for me, just you. Please, Helen. You and me, we can do it. All we need is each other."

But whatever he'd seen flash was gone, and only contempt remained. "I hate you, Howard. Do us both a favor and stay as far away from me as possible tomorrow." She turned, as if to head to her apartment, with one hand placed almost protectively on her belly. "I'm walking home alone, and if you try to follow me, I'll call the police."

He had no choice but to stand there and watch as his future, his love, and his life walked away and left him all alone.

Chapter Eighteen

With nowhere else to go, Alyssa suggested they return to the school.

It was a long, arduous walk back due to convoluted turns and doubling back an innumerable amount of times to make sure no one followed. So much so, they both questioned at different times if they even knew where they were going. Though someone might have started out following them, they were positive they arrived at the school alone.

Before leaving for the shelter, they'd placed cots in a storage closet. An acceptable risk, they decided, with little chance of discovery. Especially considering the students and most of the faculty were still on break.

"Remember when I said I would crash later?" Alyssa dropped onto a cot. "This is me crashing."

Kipling took the cot next to her and reached out his hand for hers. "I think I could sleep for two days and not move the entire time."

Alyssa gently squeezed his hand. "Do you think they got Kevan?" Though why she asked, she wasn't sure. Part of her could be happy forever being able to pretend he was safe.

"Do you really want to know what I think?" Kipling asked with a pointed look.

She thought through her response before giving it. "Yes, I think I do."

"There were gunshots fired as we left the property. I'd be shocked if he survived."

"But it's possible, right?" she asked, surprised at how hoarse she sounded.

"Yes."

She sniffled. Damn, this case was getting to her. Either that or she was going soft. She didn't like either one of those options.

She wished more than anything they weren't sleeping on cots but were sharing a bed. If they were in a bed, he would pull her close and tuck her head under his. She smiled at the realization that they had shared a bed only two times but already she knew how they would position themselves. But not tonight. She sighed.

"Come here, Alyssa," he said, rolling to his side and scooting over to give her room on the cot.

She didn't stop to ask if he was sure or if he'd have enough room. He'd offered, and she would take him up on it. Within seconds, she was in his arms and content.

The sound of a phone ringing woke them up. Alyssa guessed it to be around midmorning.

"I thought we left our phones back in the church," she said, watching Kipling take the ringing one out of his bag.

"It's a burner," he said. "Only my brothers have this number. I don't recognize who's calling." He put the phone on speaker before answering. "Hello."

"Kipling Benedict," an unfamiliar voice said. From the

way Kipling's jaw tensed and how rigid his body went, he knew exactly who it was. Somehow Alyssa knew this call was going to change everything.

"Howard Germain," Kipling replied, and Alyssa sucked in a breath. Damn, but she'd hoped she'd been wrong. "What can I do for you?"

"I was calling to see if you were interested in seeing your baby sister again?" Howard asked, and Alyssa decided he had the creepiest voice she'd ever heard.

"What kind of question is that?" Kipling demanded, and even though his voice was calm, she saw the anger in his expression. He was using all his self-control to remain calm. "Of course I want to see her."

"Excellent," Howard—or King, as she now knew he went by—said. "That's exactly the response I wanted to hear. In order to see her and get her back alive, you only have to do one thing."

Alyssa worked to make sense of the fact that this man was not only the fiend she'd been chasing because of his involvement with the local missing women, but he was also responsible for her sister's death. It was almost surreal.

"And what is that one thing?" Kipling asked.

"Bring me the police officer."

For a second, it felt as if her entire body shut down. She couldn't breathe. She couldn't move.

Kipling kept his eyes focused on her. "Why?"

Howard laughed. But it wasn't a normal laugh. It wasn't funny at all. It was scary as hell, and she knew, after only hearing it once, it would haunt her forever.

"What does it matter why I want her? You're getting your sister back. Or half sister, that is."

"I'm not willing to put my worst enemy in your hands.

Do you actually think I'm going to hand someone I care about to you?"

"Oh no, Kipling." Howard made a *tsk-tsk* sound. "Don't tell me you've grown close to the officer? The one who arrested you and made you into a laughingstock? You actually care what happens to her? It's a good thing your parents aren't here to see this. They would not approve. Honestly, between you and your brothers, you have managed to tie yourselves to the most worthless women."

"If you don't have anything else to say," Kipling said with barely contained rage, "I think it's time to end this call."

It was as if Kipling hadn't said anything. King continued talking, "I'm only saying this once. I'll be in the backyard of your beach property in Edisto tomorrow night at eight. You always talk about how important family is, and now this is your chance to prove it."

Without a word, Kipling disconnected. One look at her must have been enough for him to guess what she was thinking. "No," he said without waiting for her to say anything. "It's out of the question. Don't even think about it."

She put her hands on her hips. "When you decide to knock off the annoying mind-reading trick, let me know and we can have a reasonable conversation like two adults."

"Are you implying I'm not an adult or I'm not reasonable?" he asked.

"I'm not implying anything. I'm saying, when you assume you know what I'm going to say or do and then tell me I'm not going to do it, it's annoying. You need to stop using it as tactic to fall back on when things don't go the way you think they should."

"Is that what I'm doing?" he asked.

"No. Not at the moment. Right this second, you're just arguing with me and being a pain in the ass."

"Okay, fine. Stand right there, look me in the eye, and tell me you weren't thinking about offering yourself as a pawn to that man in order for me to get Jade back."

"You make it sound so black and white, and it isn't. I'm a trained police officer. I know how to take care of myself, how to get out of certain situations, and when I can't, I know how to fight."

"Excuse me for pointing out the obvious, but Jade has been under his care for almost all of her life. Are you going to tell me you think you know how to handle him better than she does?"

She couldn't believe that was his reasoning. "Frankly, seeing the way she looked when she came by your house that night, add in a few more weeks on the streets, and now with her guardian kidnapping her? Yes. I think I'm better prepared and equipped to handle Howard Germain than she is." She cocked her eyebrow at him again. "Truth be told, I'm probably better prepared and equipped to handle him than you are."

"Don't be ridiculous."

"Oh, excuse me. Are you going to go macho on me now? Protect me from getting my hands dirty and all that? I thought better of you." She turned to walk away, but Kipling would have no such thing.

"Don't walk away from me. I'm not finished with this conversation yet."

"Maybe not, but until you can say something worthwhile or meaningful, I'm not going to listen."

"You are the most infuriating woman ever."

"At least you found out early. Now you have time to

look for a docile Southern belle who will abide by your every whim and command."

"I have no interest in that and you know it, Alyssa."

"Not based on this conversation, I don't."

He took a step closer to her, and she swore his body hummed the way it had at his family's beach cottage right before he'd taken her down the hall to his room. "I seem to remember you were very vocal with your own commands not so long ago, weren't you?"

She told herself not to blush over anything she'd asked for in bed. "Yes, I was, and if I remember correctly, you liked it. A lot."

Somehow, he'd crossed any remaining space between them. His eyes darkened. "I fucking loved it, and you know it. I don't know what bozo told you that you should keep quiet in bed and not ask for what you want, but he was wrong. And it's time you stopped listening to him and started listening to me instead." He put his hands on her shoulders. "There is nothing sexier than a woman who knows what she wants in and out of bed and is strong enough to not only ask for it but to command it."

She lowered her voice. "Prove it. Prove to me how sexy you think it is when a woman asks for what she wants in bed."

He dipped his head low, and from all appearances, it seemed as if he was going to kiss her, but at the last moment, he turned just a tad and whispered, "For the record, I know exactly what you're doing."

She blinked her eyes and tried to look as innocent as possible. "I don't know what you're talking about."

"Don't play coy. You want to have sex, and I'm pretty much down for it whenever. But don't think for a second that I'm led so much by my dick, I don't know what you're doing." She opened her mouth to speak, but he placed a finger over her lips, cutting her off. "I can't let you do it, Alyssa. You can't go to him. I'm petrified thinking that if you do, you'll never come back."

There was a time and a place to discuss the best way to take King down, along with the pros and cons of who would be the best pawn. Right now was not the best time.

"I'm not saying I agree with you or that I won't keep pushing for the role I think I'm best suited for. However, I'm willing to agree this isn't the best time to make those decisions."

He chuckled. "Why do I feel as though you came out on top?"

"I don't know." She reached for the zipper of his pants. "But if you play your cards right, I'll let you be on top this time."

King

Thirty-three years ago
Wedding reception of Franklin and Helen

Howard had experienced bad days before, but until he stood at the front of a church and watched his best friend marry the woman he loved, he'd never known just how bad a bad day could be. At times during the ceremony he had to hold himself back so he wouldn't interrupt the minister and tell Helen in front of her obscene number of bridesmaids and ridiculous number of guests how she was minutes away from making the worst mistake of her life.

And then it was done.

The same minister he had been seconds away from interrupting was introducing Mr. and Mrs. Franklin Benedict for the first time. The bridesmaids and guests clapped.

Howard could only stand and wonder how he was going to live the rest of his life knowing Helen had married Frank and he'd been helpless to stop it from happening. He made up his mind then and there that, no matter what he had to do, he would never feel helpless again.

He did his best to abide by Helen's wish to stay away from her. It actually wasn't all that hard to do. Not only did she send him icy glares that further froze his heart, but she also ensured nothing would ever make it thaw again. In addition, anytime he got close to her, Frank was right there at her side. Holding her hand, stroking her arm, or, worse yet, kissing her.

For the first time in his life, Howard wanted nothing to do with Frank Benedict, and he wasn't sure how to make that happen because, right before graduation, Frank had asked Howard to come and work for him and his father at Benedict Industries. Howard had accepted.

He'd rationalized it by deciding that working for the Benedict family would be a good way to keep his eye on things. Like making sure Frank didn't cheat on his wife the way he had when she was his girlfriend. In other words, it gave Howard a place to wait until Helen came to her senses and filed for divorce.

The wedding director announced the newlyweds were leaving, and everyone stood to wish them well. But while the crowd threw rice at the tin-can-decorated car, Howard stood off to the side and fed rice to the birds, all the while imagining their little bellies exploding. Later he would realize that, while Frank and Helen said their goodbyes, he was ensuring a slight decrease in the pigeon population. If nothing else, at least being busy with pigeons meant he was spared having to watch Helen leave him one more time.

He looked up, and thankfully, the newlyweds had left. The festive mood started to fade. And just like that, the wedding of the century was over.

Thank goodness.

It didn't take too long for the remaining guests to begin leaving and for the crowd to thin out. He wasn't sure why he was one of the last to leave. Perhaps he had some unreasonable hope Helen would realize her mistake and come back. That on her way to whatever paradise Frank had picked out for their honeymoon, she would come to her senses and realize Howard had been right the entire time.

But of course she didn't.

After leaving the reception, he didn't feel like going back to the apartment he'd shared with Frank. Going back to his parents' house meant either twenty questions on why he was in such a piss-poor mood or, worse, when was he going to settle down. He could stomach neither.

For a while, he drove around. It was dark, and not a lot of people were out. Those that were, hurried along, driven to make it to wherever they were going as soon as possible.

That's why it was so easy for him to find her. While everybody else was running around, she was taking her time. Everyone else had somewhere they had to be, and she was content with where she was. Her laid-back pace first caught his attention. What kept it was her blonde hair and blue eyes.

Her eyes were almost the right shade, but not quite. And yet, the more he looked at her, the more he was able to convince himself it didn't matter. Especially in the dark.

In the dark, she would probably remind him of Helen.

In the dark, he probably wouldn't be able to tell the difference.

In the dark, he could do whatever he wanted.

She didn't hesitate to walk over to his car when he pulled it to a stop beside her on the road. Nor did she hesitate to get inside when he opened the door and asked where she was going.

She told him she was running away from home and he

could take her anywhere except back to where she came from.

He told her that wouldn't be a problem.

She told him her name was Rachel.

He asked if her middle name was Helen.

She was smart enough to say yes. Or stupid enough.

He still didn't want to go back to his apartment, not with memories of Helen and Frank being everywhere he looked. Especially memories of Helen.

He took Rachel Helen to a nearby hotel. He opened the car door for her in the parking lot, and the door to the hotel room. She laughed as he followed her inside.

She didn't laugh much longer.

She didn't do much of anything much longer.

As it turned out, Howard was wrong. There was no part of her that reminded him of Helen. None at all. Which is why he had to kill her.

But, of course, that was Frank's fault.

Chapter Nineteen

Kipling reluctantly rented a car the next day to take them to the Edisto property they now knew neighbored Howard's.

Alyssa appeared brave and confident at the moment, but as he'd held her last night, she confessed to being scared. Kipling told himself if she could go through doing this, he could find the strength to support her.

They didn't say anything as he drove to the beach property he'd thought only days before was so safe.

Safety, he was learning, was nothing but an illusion.

As they got closer to the beach, he couldn't stand the silence anymore. "Let's go through the plan one more time," he said.

"Must we?" she asked, sounding very tense.

He swallowed around the lump in his throat. He had a bad feeling about the day. Something told him it wasn't going to run as smoothly as they'd hoped. Of course, he told himself, what did he expect when working with a diabolical serial killer?

"No," he said in answer to her question. "We don't have

to go over it again, but it makes me feel better the more we do. Like I have control in the outcome. Of course, the truth is, I don't have control over anything."

"You may not have any control over the outcome," she said with the determination he admired so much, "but the one thing you can do is trust me and what I've been trained to do."

Her words pierced his heart with guilt. "I didn't mean in any way to imply you weren't up to the task." They had almost made it to the long drive that led to the Benedicts' beach property, but he pulled the car over because, suddenly, it became very important for him to say what he wanted to before they reached where they were going.

Alyssa looked at him as if he were crazy. "Kipling, what are you doing? Why are we stopping? You know we need to get there and get everything set up before he does."

"Yes," he said, and he actually smiled, which he wouldn't have thought possible mere moments before.

"So why did you pull the car over?" She looked at him with a raised eyebrow. "I will kick your ass into next week if this is some sort of delay tactic or if you think for one moment you're going to talk me out of doing this."

"I love you." Three words. Three *small* words, even, but while they'd felt so heavy on his tongue, now that he'd said them, he felt light and peaceful. "I love you," he said a second time because she still looked at him like he'd lost every bit of sense he ever had, and because it was so much easier to say the second time.

"Kipling." She shook her head, but before she could say anything else, he placed his finger on her lips.

"Shh," he said. "You don't need say it back. In fact I didn't say it so you'd say it back. I simply wanted you to know." He started the car back up. "Ready?"

She only nodded, but he saw the truth in her eyes. She loved him too.

* * *

Alyssa looked at her watch. One in the afternoon. King wasn't expecting them until eight, but he had to at least suspect they would show up earlier. She only hoped he wouldn't think they would be *this* early.

Even so, Kipling had parked the car at the far edge of the property so they could scope the place out. There was a chance Howard or his men would see them, but as each second ticked along silently, she couldn't help but think that chance grew smaller and smaller.

She glanced up to find Kipling looking at her, and she felt her cheeks heat before she hurriedly looked down. He loved her. Though it had seemed improbable the first time he said it, the more and more it resounded inside her head, the more and more she believed.

He. Loved. Her.

She felt a stupid grin cover her face, and she didn't even care. She turned to say something to him and almost fell down because he was right in front of her.

"Whoa," he said, placing his hands on her shoulders. "Careful there."

"I'm okay."

He kissed her cheek. "Guess what I just saw."

"What?"

"Come here." He took her hand and led her to where he'd stood moments before. "See there, in between those two trees?"

She looked to where he pointed and squinted. "Is that a treehouse?"

179

"It is. My father had it put in when we were younger. We loved it and spent hours there. It was the perfect location because you could see anyone approaching from the beach or street. Even better, they couldn't see you. I'm going to go over there and see if I can see anything. I might be able to tell where he's keeping Jade."

"I'm not sure." She started when a movement caught her eye. "What is that?"

Kipling must have spotted it as well because they both lifted their binoculars to the tree house.

"Not a what," he said. "But a who. Kevan."

The young man had obviously made it out of the shelter. He might have been in the process of doing what Kipling had suggested, looking out from the tree house to see if he could find where Jade was being held. But as they watched, a large man came up behind him. Kevan spun around, prepared to fight. Unfortunately, it was a move the large man had anticipated, because within seconds, Kevan's unconscious body was being dragged away.

King

Fifteen years ago
Homeless shelter
Charleston, South Carolina

Franklin's ex-mistress had to die. Howard didn't have an issue killing people, but it was a pity he had to get rid of this one. Frank knew how to pick them, Howard had to give the man that much. Not only young and beautiful, but she spoke with an intelligence that was both clever and witty.

At one point, Howard thought he might keep her. It had been over five years since she'd fucked Frank. If she was good, he could forgive that one sin. But then she'd done the unthinkable. She'd snooped in his office.

Contrary to popular belief, he wasn't totally without a heart. He could overlook certain things. Unfortunately, snooping was not one of those things. Snooping was borne out of lack of trust and respect. Her actions in his office proved she didn't trust or respect him. Which meant he had to kill her.

Of course, killing her brought up even more issues.

Namely, her daughter. Who just so happened to be Frank's daughter as well.

The irony of the situation was not lost on him. Franklin had always wanted a daughter. Longed for a daughter. But the Fates had not seen fit to give him one. Not a legitimate one, anyway. Instead, they had given his mistress what he'd desperately wanted. That was what Howard called poetic justice.

After killing the mistress, Howard would ensure the daughter became his. He never put much stock in daughters. He had one who was, for the most part, worthless. But Frank's little girl...

Howard grew almost giddy thinking about how he could train her and the things he would teach the Benedict bastard. Oh, yes. Unknown to anyone, he would single-handedly create the ultimate weapon to destroy the Benedicts. What better way to destroy them than with their own flesh and blood?

As it turned out, the ex-mistress wasn't Howard's only problem. Frank's favorite employee, Brock, who had been a problem for some time, was now a very big problem.

Howard walked down the hall of the building he'd set up as a homeless shelter to disguise its true purpose. What started as him wanting Helen look-alikes had turned into a profitable business when he realized he could help other men find their own Helens.

Happily married, Brock was not like the men Howard did business with. And lately it seemed the man had Frank's ear a lot more of the time than Howard did. Last weekend, Brock had flown to Seattle with Howard and Frank. From the start, Howard knew having Brock traveling with them would put a kink in his plans. Based on past trips, Frank wouldn't be a problem. As soon as they landed, his boss would check into the hotel and then, as quickly as possible, be out trying to find female companionship.

But Brock had no interest in looking for someone to fuck. Normally, the man spent time with Frank, but since Frank would be absent, that left Howard. Which meant Howard would have to be careful and watch himself around Brock.

Everything had been fine, right up until it all went to shit. Howard's Seattle contact had been able to find the most perfect Helen stand-in, a perfection that ultimately led to his current predicament. Namely, Brock happened upon Howard at an inopportune time. To be exact, he'd shown up right as Howard was teaching Not-Helen what happened when she disobeyed him.

It had all happened in a matter of seconds, but it had been enough. Enough for Howard to see the look of utter disgust in the other man's eyes. Enough for Howard to realize Brock would never see how some women had to be treated in order to make them behave properly. But worst of all, Brock had to have noticed the woman looked like she could be Helen's twin.

Unfortunately, there was already talk around the office about Howard having a crush on the boss's wife. If Brock told Frank what he'd seen, Frank would do something drastic.

So Howard had to be drastic first.

Brock had to be terminated.

The mistress, followed by Brock. Howard tightened his grip on the knife, ready to take care of the first problem.

Chapter Twenty

Alyssa and Kipling hid behind a row of anise shrubs in the backyard of Howard's property. Not long after they got in place, the man they'd watched earlier walked past with an unconscious Kevan slung over his shoulder. Neither Alyssa nor Kipling spoke until he disappeared into the nearby home.

"I'm guessing you want to follow?" Kipling asked in a whisper.

Damn straight she did. She gave a curt nod.

"Should we separate?" he asked. "Want me to check one of the other houses?"

"I don't think so. It wouldn't make sense for Howard to be operating out of multiple locations here. Since this is where Kevan's been brought, Howard's more than likely here as well."

"Makes sense."

"I think you should wait outside, though." She braced herself for his numerous reasons why that was a bad idea, but instead he surprised her.

"I don't have the training you have," he said. "I'd be more of a hinderance than help."

She nodded. "I'm not going to do anything stupid. I'll see what's going on and then come back out and call for help if I need to."

They both knew she was lying. It hurt too much to look in his eyes, so she turned and walked inside to avoid looking at him at all.

She closed the door behind her as quietly as possible and focused on the task at hand. Voices came from what seemed to be the opposite side of the house. She crept toward them.

Jade's voice was recognizable, as was a second voice, though she'd only heard it once before. She doubted she'd ever forget Howard Germain's voice. He was arguing with Jade, or at least that's what it sounded like, based on their tone.

Alyssa followed the sound down a dimly lit hallway. It felt like she was headed underground, even as she told herself the house was too close to the sea for that to be the case. The hallway curved, and voices came from a room on the right with the door open.

Alyssa pressed herself to the wall, inched as close as she dared to the opening, and turned her head to peek inside.

Jade and a man Alyssa assumed was Howard Germain stood facing each other. Jade still appeared gaunt and pale, but her arms were crossed at her chest, and there was no hiding the determined lift of her chin.

"You'll never get away with this," Jade told Howard.

"Of course I will." It wasn't until Howard took a step toward Jade that Alyssa was able to understand what was going on. Tied to a pole at the far back of the room and out of her line of sight before was Kevan. He was no longer unconscious, and his eyes grew wide when he saw her. Even though Kevan was gagged, Alyssa held a finger up to her lips. Kevan gave a slight nod.

Afraid Howard would see her, Alyssa pulled back into the hallway to decide on her next move. Kevan was tied and gagged, and if that wasn't bad enough, there was a table near Howard, its surface almost completely covered with knives. She couldn't say with absolute confidence what Howard had planned, but it couldn't be good, and she feared there wasn't time to call for help.

Before she could decide what to do, a new commotion sounded from inside the room.

"Look what we found outside," a new and gruff voice said.

Alyssa's heart sank at Howard's response. "Never one to follow directions, were you, Kipling?"

That one sentence told her everything she needed to know. Any thought she'd had about calling for help disappeared. Whatever happened was up to her.

"Officer Adams," Howard called from inside the room. "Although it's not *Officer* anymore, is it? I know you're around here somewhere. Come to me now and I won't kill the Benedict bastard immediately."

"Don't do it, Alyssa," Kipling yelled. "Run. Now, and call—"

His voice was cut off by the sound of fist hitting flesh, followed by a groan from Kipling.

Alyssa wished he hadn't yelled at her to run. Had he really expected her to leave while Howard held him, Jade, and Kevan?

"I'm coming in," she said.

"Hands empty," Howard said. "I know you're armed, but if I see a weapon, the bastard dies at once."

She put the safety on her firearm and placed it back in its holster, suddenly wishing she knew something about throwing knives. With hands up, she took a step toward the open door.

"Here I am," she said as she took the first step into the room.

She glanced around for a quick assessment. Kevan was across the room by a door that must lead to the outside. He was unguarded but gagged and bound to a pole. Two men restrained Kipling, dragging him to another pole next to Kevan. Within seconds, Kipling was likewise bound. She tried not to dwell on his swollen lip and eye. He had put up a fight.

At her right side stood Jade and Howard and the table of knives. For a fleeting second, she considered drawing her gun, but one of the men held a knife at Kipling's neck, watching her.

"Want me to restrain her, boss?" the second guy who'd been restraining Kipling asked with a nod toward Alyssa.

"No," King said. "Seeing her lover with a knife at his neck will be enough to keep her in her place."

In her place?

As much as those three words would normally infuriate her, at that moment they gave her hope. In saying them, he'd unknowingly showed his hand. He didn't see her as a threat and, based on the way he'd looked at his ward moments ago, he thought the same thing about Jade.

"Now, Jade," King said, turning his attention back to the young woman at his side. "What were you saying about me not getting away with it? Take a look around. I already have."

Jade caught Alyssa's eye. The two of them had only spoken once before, but for a second, it was as if she heard the younger woman say, *I've got this.* Alyssa gave a slight nod. Message received. The first move was Jade's, but she wasn't doing anything at the moment.

"No response?" King asked. "Have you finally remembered all I've done and commanded with a single sentence? I'm a god in this state, and no Benedict will ever better me." He chuckled, and the sound sent chills down Alyssa's spine. "Besides, why would I be the one to get away with anything? I'm not the one who's going to be doing the dirty work."

Still nothing from Jade, and that seemed to anger King more than anything.

"You think you have everything figured out," he said in an angry whisper that belied the calm facade he'd had only seconds before. "I know how you think and why you think it. Right now you think I'm going to have you kill Kevan, and in order to get through it, you've shut your mind down."

For the first time, Alyssa spied a hint of uncertainty in Jade's countenance.

King obviously noticed it as well. An evil smile curved his lips upward. "You're going to kill Kipling Benedict. Your older brother who never wanted you."

At King's words, Jade gasped and reached for the closest knife. It took a handful of seconds for Alyssa to realize Jade was hearing about her paternity for the first time.

"That's right, Jade," King said, taking a step closer and pressing his hand down on top of the knife table. "He was given everything. Everything. And you had nothing. He's a selfish, good-for-nothing bastard who only cares for himself and his net worth. The world will be better off without him. Throw the knife and end him."

Alyssa watched, ready to grab her gun if needed. She didn't think Jade would kill Kipling, no matter how surprised she was to hear of their relation. Even as the young woman drew back the knife, with her eyes focused on her newly discovered brother, Alyssa didn't reach for her weapon. But it wasn't until the second before the knife struck that it became clear what her target was.

Moving as if the knife was an extension of herself, Jade gracefully plunged it down and through King's hand, pinning him to the table.

Too caught up in watching Kipling, King didn't notice until too late where the knife was headed. When it struck, his scream was bloodcurdling.

"No," was all Jade said. "Find someone else to kill for you. I quit."

Chapter Twenty-One

The room broke into complete pandemonium.

King continued yelling but didn't attempt to remove the knife. One of his men ran to his side. The other went for Jade. Alyssa didn't hesitate before running to Kipling and removing the gag. He said something to her, but she couldn't make out what. At the time, she assumed it was because of how intensely she was focused on freeing him. It wasn't until the last of the bonds fell away and she had to catch him before he dropped to the floor that she realized his injuries were worse than she'd originally assumed.

"Kipling?" she asked as he struggled to get his footing.

"Sorry." His voice was laced with pain. "I think they broke a rib and maybe my ankle?"

She eased him to where he was sitting on the ground. Getting medical help would have to wait until she took care of King and his men. Glancing around, she reached for her gun, but right when she almost touched it, it was pulled away. Surprised, she rocked back to land on her butt, yelping in surprise.

"Good job," King told whoever had stopped her. The

hand Jade had stabbed was wrapped with a cloth. Jade herself stood at his side, restrained by the larger of his two men. "Bring those two, and you, bring the bastard girl. I'm ready to end this once and for all."

"What about him?" The guy holding Alyssa's hands behind her back asked with a nod toward Kevan.

"I'll take care of him," King said.

With both her arms pulled behind her, there was no way to fight her captor. Alyssa tried kicking him, but he only laughed and told her she would have to try harder. *I'm sorry,* she mouthed to Kevan as she was dragged past him.

"I'll come back for the guy," her captor said. "From the looks of it, he isn't going to be causing anyone any trouble anytime soon."

A quick glance proved he was right. Kipling was curled up on his side, where she'd left him, his eyes closed and his breathing labored.

"I don't care what it looks like," King countered. "He's a Benedict. Don't turn your back to him."

Alyssa and Jade were led to a small cell-like room down the hall, where they were tied to the wall. The room had only the one door and no windows, which meant little chance to escape. Alyssa hoped their legs wouldn't be tied, but as soon as Kipling was brought into the room, her ankles were tied together, as were Jade's. She didn't spend too much time lamenting the loss of her feet, though; she was too busy focusing on Kipling. From what she could tell, he still hadn't opened his eyes.

King's two hired men left, and Howard stood in the middle of the room, looking at the three of them with uncontrolled glee. "Isn't this the strangest family reunion you've ever seen? You have the unwanted bastard, the unknown aunt, and the current head of the family. I tell you what, I have a few things to get set up. You three say your goodbyes, and I'll be back in few minutes."

Alyssa kept telling herself, this couldn't be it. She didn't feel like she was moments away from death. But the more she thought about it, the faster her heart went and the clammier she felt. A glance at Jade offered her no insight as to what her niece felt.

She hadn't allowed herself to think of Jade as her niece until that moment.

Her chest felt tight. How could she lose her niece when she'd just found her?

"Aunt?" Jade asked. "And he's my brother?"

"I only discovered the truth a few days ago." How was it possible it felt more like years than days?

"Is he gone?" Kipling cracked one eye open.

"Kipling." Alyssa could have wept with relief at seeing him lucid. "Oh, thank goodness. How are you feeling?"

"Like shit." He turned his head toward Jade. "I know it probably doesn't mean much at this point, but I'm sorry, Jade. I wish I had known."

Jade shrugged.

Undeterred by her lack of emotion, he kept talking. "I always wanted a sister. Don't get me wrong, I love Keaton and Knox, and I can't imagine life without them, but I always felt something was missing. I know now it was you."

Something flashed in Jade's eyes. "I think deep down I knew all along but never allowed myself to believe it. And now I have an aunt too. All my life it's just been me." She looked to Alyssa. "My mother was your sister?"

"Yes." Alyssa smiled. "I can see her in you. Obviously, your most stunning feature is the Benedict eyes you share with your brothers, but I see your mom in the shape of your nose and the way you hold your head."

Jade's eyes looked wet. "I don't remember her hardly at all."

"When we get out of here, I'll tell you anything you want to know about her."

"If you have a plan on how to get us out," Kipling said, "now would be a great time to fill us in."

"And Kevan," Jade whispered. "He doesn't deserve this. He was only trying to help."

Alyssa thought Kevan was probably either dead or close to it, but answered only, "I'll do my best. I wish I had a plan, but I've got nothing."

"Do you think you can reach inside my front pocket if we shift around a little?" Jade asked Alyssa. "I have some things that might be useful. If they're still in there."

Alyssa starting shifting, trying to get close enough.

"I swiped a key from one of the guards a few days ago," Jade said. "It might fit on these chains. It's in one pocket. I have a throwing star in my back pocket. I only got it a few minutes ago when I lifted it from the knife table without anyone seeing."

Alyssa worked harder. She had to get the key before Howard came back in. Had to. She pulled it out of Jade's pocket seconds before the door to the small room opened and Howard walked in, holding a gun.

"Time's up," he said. "I have a private jet on its way to take me out of the country. I hope you've all said your piece."

Chapter Twenty-Two

Alyssa had never seen another person look so deranged and devoid of anything resembling humanity. She hoped she had enough time to free her hands before he started shooting.

"I was down the hall, trying to decide who I wanted to shoot first, when I realized it would be more fun for you guys to decide." He pointed the gun at Jade. "Should it be the lost little sister no one cared enough about to find?" He pressed the barrel of the gun against her forehead. "Guess who cares if I shoot you? No one. I could shoot you dead right here and now and I bet no one would even cry."

He held the gun still for a long moment. Alyssa was pretty sure no one dared breathe, though she worked as much as possible to unlock her arms. She stopped suddenly when Howard swung around and aimed the gun in her direction.

"Or should I shoot the unknown aunt? It's a sad story when you think about it. The young girl who loved history. Loved it so much and from such an early age that there was never any doubt in her mind about what she wanted to do with her life. She wanted to immerse herself in history. Read about it. Write about it. Study it. Learn all she could about it and then teach others about it."

Alyssa gasped. How did he know all that? It wasn't like it was public knowledge.

"But then your sister shows up dead, and no one could figure out who killed her. You made a promise to yourself not only that would you never stop looking until you solved your sister's case but that you wouldn't rest until there were no more cold cases. An admirable goal, but you had to let history go, didn't you?"

Alyssa lifted her chin, refusing to let him get to her. And yet the gun was still pointed at her.

"What a miserable life. Unable to do what you wanted because of a promise you made as a child? Of course, we can't forget your true shining moment. How for years you slept with a serial kidnapper and killer. I, for one, love the irony, but it's probably distressing to you. I'd probably be doing you a favor by shooting you."

Alyssa's body shook. She fully expected him to pull the trigger, which was why she was so shocked when he stepped away and took aim at Kipling.

"Then maybe, I tell myself, I should cut off the head first. The mighty Benedict firstborn and heir. But even I know that's not a good enough reason to kill someone. Surely, if I think hard enough, I can think of a reason to not only justify killing you, but also for shooting you first. And then I remember that you're the reason for every-thing. Every life ruined, every life taken comes back to you."

It was such a preposterous statement, Alyssa stopped working the key in order to listen. Kipling didn't say anything, but she saw the confusion in his eyes. Even Jade looked surprised. Odd, Alyssa thought her niece knew just about everything pertaining to King and his motives.

"You were conceived before your parents were married," Howard continued, still not making sense. What did that have to do with anything?

"Your mother knew she was expecting." Howard nearly rambled, and excitement seemed to pulse through him at being able to explain. "When I approached her the night before her wedding and begged her to run away with me, she wouldn't do it because of you. So you see, if it hadn't been for you, Helen would have been mine and none of this"—he swept his arm—"would have had to happen. That means it's all your fault. Funny how I always blamed your dad, but he's not the real culprit. The real problem is you."

Howard looked from Kipling to Alyssa to Jade. "I don't care which one of you dies first, but I'm not going to decide. Jade, give me a number."

Jade didn't hesitate. "Fuck you."

Howard took aim at her. "Last warning."

Jade lifted her chin. "Fuck. You."

Howard shot her in her leg. "Give me a number."

Alyssa was shocked the young woman didn't cry out. Only a few tears on her cheeks showed she was even hurt. "Jade," Alyssa said. "He's going to kill us all. Give him what he wants."

Howard actually smiled. "That might be the smartest thing I've ever heard you say."

"And no matter what," Alyssa said, doing her best to tune him out, "I'm thrilled to be your aunt. I want you in my family very much." She had rolled herself so Howard couldn't see her mouth, but Jade could. Hoping the young woman understood, she mouthed, *I'm free. Go big,* and nodded.

Jade addressed Howard, "Nine hundred ninety-nine thousand."

Alyssa was willing to bet King's face was priceless. As it was, he sounded totally out of character when he replied, "What was that?"

"That was my number," Jade explained.

It was the opening Alyssa was waiting for. "It's a ridiculous number, Jade," she said. "You should have picked something like three. You can count that. You can't count nine hundred ninety-nine thousand. I mean, seriously, try it." This was it. The only chance of escape. "One. Two. Three."

Alyssa had a slight jump on King. It wasn't until she hit three that he realized something was up and she wasn't only counting to show Jade what a ridiculous number she'd picked. But by that time, Alyssa had already acted. Having unlocked herself seconds before, when she counted three, she rolled over and reached for Jade's back pocket. Jade shifted slightly, allowing her access. In one move, Alyssa grabbed the throwing star, hurled it at the hand King held the gun with, the one Jade hadn't stabbed, and rolled them both out of the way of potential bullets.

King howled. Hoping against hope that she had struck him, Alyssa risked a glance. He no longer held the gun but had dropped it to the ground.

Alyssa lunged forward, and Howard's face turned a brilliant shade of red when he realized he wouldn't reach the gun before she did. He kicked out a foot, making contact with Alyssa's wrist seconds after she grabbed the weapon. Gritting her teeth, she rolled away from him, lifted the gun, and shot him between the eyes.

It seemed like everything shifted to slow motion as his body first jerked backward and then fell forward. Alyssa thought he was dead, but she rose to her feet to check. Satisfied that no one would be alive following a gunshot to the brain, she dropped beside Jade and unchained her first.

"We need to get out of here and find Kevan, quickly, before those other two men show up." Alyssa didn't understand why Jade wasn't moving faster. Didn't she know they weren't out of danger yet?

Jade rubbed her wrist where the bindings had been while Alyssa went to work to unlock Kipling. "We'll probably find their bodies somewhere in the building," Jade said.

"You think he killed them?" Alyssa asked.

Jade nodded. "He told us he was planning to leave the country, right? If that's the case, he wouldn't leave anyone behind. It was never his plan to leave anyone alive."

"How about the pilot?"

"Unless he's changed a lot in a short amount of time, he never had a personal pilot. I imagine it's the same charter service he's always used."

That was at least one thing to feel good about. She quickly unchained Kipling, growing more and more concerned with each second that passed. His eyes looked glassy again, and worse yet, his speech was slurred when he spoke.

"Is it over?" he asked. "Because, all of a sudden, I don't feel so good."

Alyssa called his name over and over as he lost consciousness.

Chapter Twenty-Three

Alyssa paced back and forth across the floor of the hospital waiting room.

Kipling had been in surgery for several hours. No one was telling her anything about his condition, and she couldn't imagine anything worse. But then again they weren't telling his family anything, either. They had all showed up: Keaton and Tilly, Knox and Bea. Even Maggie. Only to be told absolutely nothing, other than that Kipling had been alive when he arrived at the hospital.

Before leaving the beach, they called in officers from an adjoining county. Jade had been right, and they found the bodies of the two men who'd restrained them in the hallway. Both with their throats cut.

Kevan had been more fortunate. He'd had the sense of mind to play dead, and King had obviously fallen for the ruse. Currently, Kevan was being held for observation in the hospital, but all signs pointed to his being released soon.

Jade herself had been relatively quiet since returning from having her leg looked at. She spoke to no one. Choosing instead to sit in the corner of the hospital waiting room. Alone. Just as Alyssa suspected she had spent most of her life. That would change and, she hoped, soon.

At the moment, everybody was too worried about Kipling to think about much of anything else. Alyssa felt sick with the uncertainty of it all.

It was another hour before anybody cracked open the door to their waiting room. When the doctor entered the room, he looked tired, like he'd just fought in mighty battle.

He looked around, quietly taking them all in. "Benedict family?" he asked, with no emotion in his voice at all except for fatigue.

As the second oldest, Knox stood and took a step forward. "Yes," he said. "We're all Benedicts here."

The doctor nodded toward a group of chairs that looked like they could handle them all. "Let's have a seat."

Alyssa prayed it wasn't as bad as she feared and took several deep breaths after sitting down. Someone nudged her hand, and she looked down to find it was Jade. Her niece gave her a careful smile but, for the most part, looked unsure. Alyssa wanted nothing more than to pull her close in a tight hug but was afraid that would scare her, so she settled for squeezing her hand.

"Mr. Benedict has many severe internal injuries," the doctor continued. "The next twenty-four hours are going to be the most critical, but everything looks good. There's no reason not to expect a full recovery."

A collective sigh of relief came over the group.

"When can we see him?" Knox asked.

"I know you all want to see him, but let's keep it calm for right now. He needs to rest. Keep it to two at a time."

Knox nodded.

The doctor stood. "I'll let the nurse know to come get you when he's settled."

They moved as a group back to the other section of the waiting room. Alyssa kept holding Jade's hand, since her niece didn't seem in a hurry to pull it away. She wasn't sure who was more surprised, her or her niece, when Tilly walked over to them and took a seat beside Jade.

Alyssa knew Tilly was a sweetheart, but she also knew that out of all the Benedicts, Tilly had always had a major problem with Jade. Alyssa looked around, attempting to catch Keaton's eye and perhaps get a feel for what his fiancée was thinking. But at the moment, he was talking to Maggie.

Alyssa told herself she didn't have to tell Tilly that now was not the time to have a long, drawn-out discussion. But Tilly's smile was friendly, and Alyssa felt herself relax.

"You know," Tilly said, "I don't think I ever thanked you for helping Keaton with the secret passage. I might not be here today if it wasn't for you. Thank you."

Alyssa discovered at that moment that Jade had a beautiful smile.

Thankfully, it wasn't long before the nurse came to escort them in to see Kipling. They let Alyssa go by herself, and for that she would be forever thankful.

She pulled a chair over to his bed and sat down. He was sleeping, and she didn't want to wake him but she had to touch him. His left hand was above the covers and was one of the few parts of him that wasn't either bruised or stabbed with a needle.

She took hold of his left hand and studied it, remembered how, a few short nights ago, that same hand had loved her. The words hadn't been said between them, but their bodies knew. She stroked her fingers from the top of his wrist, across his knuckles, and down to his fingertips.

"I can't believe how close we came to dying," she said,

knowing he probably couldn't hear her. "All I can think about now is how horrible it would have been if I'd died without telling you I love you." She sniffled and dropped her head. "I love you, Kipling. I'm sorry I didn't say it before."

He squeezed her hand, and she gasped when she looked up and saw him smiling.

"You're awake," she said.

"You don't have to apologize for not saying you loved me before," he said. "You do, however, have to remember who said it first."

Chapter Twenty-Four

Two weeks later, Kipling felt as if things were finally returning to normal at Benedict House and Benedict Industries. Following the death of Howard, and Kipling's and Kevan's releases from the hospital, the entire family had been going off in several different directions.

As it turned out, Kevan was a journalist who had been working undercover for King in order to collect enough evidence to bring him down. Apparently, a childhood friend of his went missing shortly after she started to work for King. Though, to date, he hadn't found any information on her, he'd discovered most of the missing documents concerning Mr. Brock.

To no one's surprise, Howard had planted all the evidence that ensured the collapse of the Brock family. Kipling did everything he could to publicly exonerate Tilly's father but knew he could never come close to making it up to her. Fortunately, Tilly had her parents' forgiving spirit and refused to allow the past to color her future.

Knox and Bea had worked with Kevan to pull all the files together. It had taken a lot of man hours to go through everything from not only what Kevan had found but also the files discovered recently at Benedict House.

With that arduous task completed, the newlyweds were spending their time renovating their beach house. Bea had recently decided against running for Congress, and though Kipling was glad the couple would be staying local, he didn't look forward to everyone moving out of Benedict House. Keaton and Tilly had plans to start looking for their own place soon.

Kipling had hoped Jade would stay at Benedict House, but she'd moved in with Alyssa. As much as he wanted to get to know his sister, he recognized the relationship would take time. Besides, he would never do or say anything to hinder the bond he saw growing between aunt and niece.

Alyssa hadn't tried to get her old job back at the police department. She'd surprised him the day before by telling him she was thinking about going back to school for a history degree. He thought that was a wonderful idea.

"Kipling?"

Speaking of the love of his life...

"In the sunroom," he called to Alyssa. She'd been out with Jade, and he was anxious to hear how everything went.

He gave his woman a quick kiss when she came into the room. "Where's my sister?" he asked, looking over Alyssa's shoulder.

"She's right outside. Said she had to make a phone call." Alyssa sat down on the nearby couch. "I'm pretty certain it was to Kevan. He's been by the house every night this week."

"Do I need to have a man-to-man with him?"

"Hell no. Those two have been through hell, and they're both mature enough to make up their own minds."

Kipling chuckled. "Just checking. How did the will reading go?"

They had all been stunned when an attorney from New York contacted Jade a few days ago asking for her to be present for the reading of Howard's will. He indicated that he'd be flying into South Carolina today if she'd be able to meet with him.

"It wasn't anything like I expected," Alyssa said. "We were the only ones there."

"What? I thought Howard was married?"

Alyssa shook her head. "Divorced. Three years ago. Apparently she discovered a few of his side businesses, drained her personal bank account, and left without a word. Sent the divorce papers via a courier."

"Damn." Kipling whistled. "So if you were the only people there..."

"Yes," Alyssa replied to his unasked question. "He left her everything."

Before Kipling could say anything, the doorbell rang, and within seconds, footsteps sounded down the hallway. They both turned and were surprised to see Jade walking behind Maggie. The housekeeper looked all out of sorts.

"If I've told this girl once, I've told her a thousand times, she doesn't have to ring the doorbell. That's what the key you gave her is for." Maggie took a deep breath and pointed to Kipling. "Don't make me do it."

"Do what?" Jade asked, watching the older woman turn around and walk away.

"Nothing," Kipling said. "She's all talk."

Alyssa raised an eyebrow at him because she knew better, but Kipling gave a fake cough and looked at Jade. "How are you doing?"

"Okay. I thought about refusing it at first." Jade walked

over to a large-cushioned armchair and sat down. "But now I've decided to keep it and use the money to open a home or halfway house or something." She looked up with the smile that was coming easier and easier every day. "You know, something that he would have despised but that I could do a lot of good with?"

"That's a grand idea," Kipling said. "In fact, you may want to speak with Keaton and Tilly. You might be able to start it under the Benedict Community Development Division."

"Yes!" Jade laughed. "That would have pissed him off even more."

"Jade," Alyssa said, "make sure this is something you *want* to do and not something you're doing out of spite. Opening that sort of property is a wonderful idea, but you don't want your life's work to be dictated by hate."

"Too much of my life has already been dictated by hate," Jade said. "This is something I feel called to do. The fact that King would hate it just makes it an even better idea."

Jade

One month later

It's easy to feel comfortable around Alyssa. Almost as soon as we escaped from King's place, she felt like family. It's been harder with the Benedict side. It's nothing they've done, though. I think they truly have no idea how intimidating they all are. Especially when they're all together.

Kevan gets me. At first I thought it was nothing deeper than the connection we both had to King, but now I think it's more. He's more. We're more. I've never had a boyfriend before, but I'm excited, and Alyssa answers any questions I have without making me feel stupid for having them.

I pull my car up to Benedict House. It's actually Alyssa's car, but she's been letting me drive it. As I walk to the side door the family uses, the unease I usually feel approaching the house is missing. Without questioning if it's something I should do or not, I use the key Kipling gave me weeks ago and let myself in. The only reason I can think of for why I do so is that I'm excited about what I want to show them.

Everyone has gathered in the living room, Keaton and Tilly, Knox and Bea, Kipling and Alyssa. Even Maggie is sitting with them, but when she sees me, she jumps up and hugs me, mumbling something about finally using my key.

"You've made her whole year," Keaton whispers to me when she lets me go, and I sit down beside him. Of my three older brothers, I feel the most comfortable around Keaton. It makes sense, as he's the one I'm around the most. Kipling was right, Keaton and Tilly loved the idea of the center I proposed and have been helping me make it a reality.

"Was it ready?" Tilly whispers from Keaton's other side.

I nod in reply, and when she raises an eyebrow, a silent way to ask if I need help, I shake my head.

Everyone's watching me with excitement in their eyes. Not for the first time, I'm slightly taken aback by the realization that this is my family.

"You guys know about the center I'm working on." I pull out my phone. "I got a message this morning telling me the sign was ready. I went by to get a picture so I could show you." I turn the screen so everyone can see, but my focus is on my aunt.

Alyssa's hand flies to her mouth. "Jade..." she starts, but gets choked up. Kipling puts an arm around her. "I love it," she finally says, unable to move her gaze away from the picture of the sign.

THE ALLISON GRANT SAFE HOUSE

"Perfect," Kipling adds, and the others murmur in agreement.

Bea passes Alyssa a tissue. "I can't think of a better memorial for your mother and Alyssa's sister."

Bea's been helping out with the legal steps involved

with the center, and I'm so grateful. I try not to dwell on how differently things might have turned out if I hadn't gone to her office that night I did.

"I didn't know her last name was Grant," Knox says.

"King didn't either, at first," I say. "That's why he didn't know Alyssa was my aunt. The different last names."

Alyssa nods. "Allison kept our biological dad's name, but my mother had mine changed when my stepdad adopted me."

"I'll never forget standing there and hearing Howard say he'd never be bested by a Benedict." I smile at the memory. "I can't believe he was actually right about something. He was brought down by an Adams."

"Semantics," Kipling silences the entire room by saying. "She'll be a Benedict. I was just waiting for the right time to ask."

Taking advantage of the relatively rare quiet moment, Kipling stands, turns to face the stunned woman at his side, and gets down on one knee. "I've been wanting to do this since we left the hospital, and I've had this in my pocket every day for the past two weeks in case the perfect moment arrived. However, I have to say, I never pictured it going quite like this." He reaches into his pocket and pulls out a stunning solitaire diamond ring. "Alyssa Adams, will you marry me?"

Tears are rolling down Alyssa's cheeks again. "Yes."

She barely gets the word out before the ring is on her finger, and he pulls her into his arms and kisses her.

I've known for a week about the ring and how Kipling wanted to propose when Alyssa least expected it. From all appearances, everything had worked out perfectly.

Which is why I'm confused when Kipling pulls away and addresses me.

"I've been talking with our family attorney and if you want—and I hope you do—he has papers prepared to change your name to Benedict and, at my request, Maggie has been supervising the renovation of some guest rooms for you. We want you as part of our family. Never doubt it."

It's what I've wanted forever but never allowed myself to believe possible. "Yes," I manage to say.

Kipling leans over to whisper Alyssa's ear, but we all hear, anyway. "I've already cleared most of my stuff out of my closet if you'd like to move in for a forever or two."

"I think that's a rather remarkable deal, Mr. Benedict. I accept."

"Best one I've ever made or will ever make," he says before kissing her again.

Epilogue 1

The following scene was only found in the print edition of *Broken Promise*. It has been rewritten and reedited for *Exposed Desire*.

Christmas Eve
Benedict House

Kipling Benedict seemed to have lost his bride.

A bad enough problem on its own, but when added to the fact that today was his wedding day *and* that his brothers thought his predicament was the most hilarious thing ever?

"Seriously, Kip?" Keaton asked, though the smile on his face was huge. "You already ran her off? It hasn't even been twenty-four hours yet. I thought for sure you'd at least make it forty-eight."

"My bet was twelve," Knox said with an identical smile. "I didn't have her lasting through the wedding night."

His youngest brother opened his mouth to say more, but Tilly took his hand and told him to be nice.

Kipling discreetly excused himself from the small party of guests still lingering at Benedict House. It had only been about three months since everything had gone down at the beach. Neither he nor Alyssa had wanted a big wedding. Instead, they'd wanted a day to focus on themselves and their love, not a big production.

The ceremony itself had been held in a local church a few hours before and had been so emotional that very few of those present left with dry eyes. Even Jade, Alyssa's maid of honor, had cried.

The reception at Benedict House was perfect. All in all, it had been a wonderful day. Except for the fact Alyssa was nowhere to be seen.

Kipling went around the house, looking. The thing was, he knew Alyssa better than anybody, and he knew she hadn't run out on him. Not after everything they'd been through and everything they nearly lost.

If he had to guess, his wife had needed to go somewhere quiet for a moment. To get away from the hustle and bustle, to breathe for a minute. She was so very much like him in that manner. He had learned out of necessity to ignore that part of himself, but she hadn't, and he'd do whatever it took to ensure she never did.

Suddenly, he knew exactly where to find her.

Kipling walked down the stairs and to the end of the hall to their favorite room. The sunroom. In the summer, it was his favorite place to rest, to think, and to just be quiet. In the winter, especially around Christmas, the room became magical. Since it was Christmas Eve, he had a feeling he knew where to find his wife.

She didn't hear him approaching, so he stood for a few seconds and watched her. She was, of course, beautiful. She still had her wedding gown on, and she looked like the queen she now was. Sexy. Awe-inspiring. Regal. All those and more. That was his bride. His wife. His everything.

Currently, she was looking out the window. The one next to the Christmas tree she stood beside. The white lights on the tree gave everything a romantic glow, and he almost laughed. Ten minutes ago, he would have made a bet that the day could not have gotten more romantic. It appeared he was wrong.

Before he could speak, she saw his reflection in the window and laughed softly. "Let me guess, Keaton is already bugging you about losing your wife?"

With hands shoved in his pockets, he moved to stand next to her. Once there, he brushed away a piece of wayward hair and kissed the spot just under her ear. The one that drove her wild. "Yes, even after I told him there was nothing you could've found out about me that would have made you leave."

Because she knew all his secrets and loved him anyway.

"His wedding with Tilly is next June," she said. "Let's think up ways to get him back." She turned and gave him the grin that was only for him. The one he felt in his very soul.

"I always knew you were my better half, and now I know it for a fact. You're just as devious as I am. It's actually even worse from you because nobody would expect it."

She would claim she wasn't devious at all, even though he thought she knew better. In fact, he was certain she knew the truth. She was much more devious than he was, she just didn't want to argue tonight.

He leaned down gave her a soft kiss before whispering in her ear, "If you aren't running away from me, what are you doing all by yourself?"

"I thought you would've known," she said. "I was waiting for you."

He wrinkled his forehead. "You were? Whatever for?"

"It's our wedding day, right?"

"Yes," he said because she seemed to be waiting for an answer.

"And tomorrow's Christmas?"

"Yes," he said again.

"I need to give you your present."

"Now?" he asked.

She nodded. "I have one for you tomorrow, but this one is extra special, and I needed to tell you tonight."

"Oh?"

"I went to the doctor yesterday."

He frowned; she had been tired lately. They had both chalked it up to wedding preparations, moving her stuff to

Benedict House, and the holidays. He hadn't known it was so bad she needed a doctor. Nor could he understand why she hadn't told him. "You did?"

"Yes," she replied.

He cleared his throat. "I don't want to be overbearing or anything, but in the future, I need to know if you're so sick you have to go to the doctor."

She still wore that soft smile. "Absolutely. In fact, it just so happens there will be lots of doctor visits in my future."

His heart threatened to stop and he took hold of her shoulders, gently. "My god, Alyssa. Are you that sick?"

"I'm not sick at all." She must have recognized he had no clue what was going on because she added, "Daddy."

There was a strange buzzing sound in his ears, and he felt himself smile as the word sunk in. "Say that again."

This time, she took his hand and placed it over her still-flat belly. "Daddy."

He didn't try to stop the tears as he took his wife in his arms and whispered how happy he was and how much he loved her.

It appeared he hadn't lost his wife after all. He had, in fact, gained the world.

Epilogue 2

I don't plan to write more Benedicts books, but I can't help
but wonder how things are going for the characters.
The following snippet has never before been published and
is really just a fun little scene that popped into my head
one day.

I hope it makes you smile.

Two years later
Charleston, South Carolina

Ruth didn't care what the sign in the yard said; there was no way the building in front of her was a safe house. It was too new and too nice. She reached up to wipe the sweat from her forehead and grimaced when she unintentionally smelled herself. Even if it was the right place, it was doubtful they'd take in someone as smelly as she was.

When was the last time she'd taken a shower? How pathetic was it that she couldn't remember? Hot tears of shame prickled her eyes, and she took deep, even breaths, telling herself she *was not* going to cry in the middle of a residential section of Charleston, South Carolina.

She should keep moving, but the woman who worked at the last shelter she'd stayed at in Columbia had gone on and on about the new Allison Grant House. Hearing her talk about it had made it sound so perfect. Ruth hadn't realized how much she'd looked forward to it until it didn't seem like an option anymore.

The woman had smiled while talking about the place, and that one thing alone captured Ruth's attention. Who smiled about a safe house? But the lady in Columbia wouldn't stop talking, explaining how residents were able to enroll in a nearby community college, work toward their GED, or be paired with someone from the community for in-depth, on-the-job training.

Ruth had questioned how anyone could afford so much, and the lady had simply said, "Oh, honey. It's owned and operated by the Benedicts." As if that fact alone explained everything. Maybe it had. No one else listening seemed to doubt the Benedicts' ability to pull off such an amazing program.

Unfortunately, Ruth was certain that, with programs that amazing, there had to be a massive waiting list. Not only that, but she'd also heard nightmares about the lengthy interview processes at other safe houses. One girl at a shelter in Georgia had been told she'd have to sleep with the director to get a spot in his coveted house.

Hell, she'd have been better off staying with her stepfather.

Ruth had very nearly decided to turn around when a voice beside her asked, "Do you need a place to stay?"

Ruth turned to see who had the nerve to ask such a direct question, but her comeback died on her lips when she saw the young woman standing to her side.

The woman was close to Ruth's age and wore jeans and a T-shirt. Her eyes were an odd color, but what stuck Ruth the most about them was the way they seemed to imply that, once before, the stranger had been exactly where Ruth was now. *She must be a resident of the safe house.*

Ruth let herself relax a bit and nodded toward the still-imposing building. "I heard a lot good things about this place. But I didn't think it'd be so uppity looking. They must have a line of people waiting to get in."

"You never know." The woman motioned for Ruth to follow her. "Come on. I'll go with you."

"Thanks," Ruth said. If a resident showed up with her, maybe they'd be more likely to give her a room.

They walked silently toward the entrance of the safe house. Ruth looked over her shoulder out of habit, checking to ensure no one was watching. It had been six months. She'd have thought she'd have stopped looking by now, but no. Part of her always expected to find her stepfather or stepbrother waiting for her in every new city. Even now, the mere thought made her heart pound.

She told herself she wasn't going to think of them anymore and hurried to catch up with the woman in front of her. In a matter of seconds, they walked through the front door, and an odd sense of security wrapped itself around Ruth. She actually felt safe for the first time in she didn't know how long.

The inside of the house was just as surprising as the outside. Ruth had been in numerous places over the past six months, but this was the only one that didn't feel like an institution. Quite the opposite, in fact. Simply walking through the foyer, Ruth had a sense of belonging, and the various blue hues filled her with a feeling of peace she'd not thought possible moments before.

Several people waved at her guide, yet they stopped for no one, continuing through the foyer, skirting what appeared to be a living room, and down a hall of offices. The door at the end was open, and that's the one the woman stepped into, without even knocking. Shocked but not wanting to stop, Ruth followed.

It was a beautiful corner office with windows overlooking a massive garden. The office's occupant, who Ruth assumed was the director, sat at the desk. At their entry, she looked up and smiled.

"Jade," she said, and the name sounded familiar to Ruth, but she couldn't place it. "Did you and Kevan have a nice lunch?" She held her hand up. "On second thought, don't answer that. You're late, so it's probably TMI."

The director was a beautiful woman, made even more so by the peaceful contentment that seemed to cover her entire body. She stood up, and Ruth couldn't help but gawk at the hugely pregnant belly she'd not seen while the woman had been sitting.

"If you two will excuse me," she said, "Kip and I are going to drop Grant off with Bea and Knox, and then the two of us are having an afternoon and evening to ourselves before this one arrives. We're having dinner at the farmers market. I swear I plan to eat my weight in brussels sprouts."

Jade made a gagging noise, and the pregnant woman laughed as she came around the desk. She gave Jade a quick hug, smiled and nodded to Ruth, and was off.

Shaking her head, Jade slipped behind the desk and waved to a chair. "Welcome to the Allison Grant House. I'm Jade Benedict."

Benedict. That was a name she recognized. The name that seemed to have superpowers attached to it. And yet...

Ruth looked over her shoulder at the door the other woman had just walked out and then back to Jade. Her mind tried to work out what had just happened.

Jade must have picked up on her confusion. "Sorry, that was my aunt, Alyssa Benedict. She steps in sometimes when I'm out."

Ruth couldn't help but gape. "You're the director?"

Jade only nodded, and really, she didn't have to explain. She just looked so young to Ruth, yet the more she looked at her, the more she thought she saw. And she had a feeling Jade had seen and experienced more in her life than many people who were three times her age.

"In that case." Ruth sat down in the nearby chair. "I need a place to stay."

"You're aware that we do more than give you a handout and a place to stay? You'll sign an agreement signifying you will either be in school or work for the time you reside here."

"I can go to college?" Ruth whispered.

"Community college to start, but yes."

Ruth closed her eyes as tears threatened to fall. She hadn't thought college to be possible after her mom died. Not with her stepfather still living. He'd thought it ridiculous for females to attend high school, much less anything beyond.

"Yes," she said in reply. "I'd love nothing more than to have the chance to go."

"I believe I know how you feel," Jade said with a soft smile. "Are you pregnant or is there any chance you may be pregnant?" She hesitated before continuing, "I know that's very personal, but if you are, we'll set you up with a doctor to ensure you and your child are as healthy as possible. If you have any children traveling with you, they may stay with you here. We have separate dormitories for expectant mothers and mothers with children."

Ruth shook her head. "I'm not pregnant, and I don't have anyone traveling with me."

Jade typed something on her laptop. "I'll need the name you want listed on our official records. Off the record, if, at some time in future, you'd like for us to run a search on a different name, just let me know."

Ruth wasn't sure she understood at all. Was this woman telling her it was okay if she lied about her name?

Jade leaned closer. "I understand you need time to see that we're trustworthy. Giving your real name, especially if you're on the run from someone, is a huge step."

Yes, Jade understood exactly. In fact, Ruth rarely gave anyone her real name. The difference here was, wasn't Jade opening herself up to an attack or some sort of danger by being so slack about the whole thing?

Ruth shrugged. "I appreciate that, but I don't see how

you're not making yourself vulnerable by allowing people to use a fake name."

Something flashed in Jade's eyes, and her voice dropped. "The last person who thought I was vulnerable ended up with a knife pinning his hand to a table."

About the Author

Even though she graduated with a degree in science, Tara knew she'd never be happy doing anything other than writing. Specifically, writing love stories.

She started with a racy BDSM story and found she was not quite prepared for the unforeseen impact it would have. Nonetheless, she continued and The Submissive Series novels would go on to be both *New York Times* and *USA Today* bestsellers. One of those, THE MASTER, was a 2017 RITA finalist for Best Erotic Romance. Over one million copies of her books have been sold worldwide.

www.tarasueme.com

Also by Tara Sue Me

THE SUBMISSIVE SERIES:

The Submissive

The Dominant

The Training

The Chalet*

Seduced by Fire

The Enticement

The Collar

The Exhibitionist

The Master

The Exposure

The Claiming*

The Flirtation

Mentor's Match

The Mentor & The Master*

Top Trouble

Nathaniel's Gift*

The Pretender*

The Anniversary*

RACK ACADEMY SERIES:

Master Professor

Headmaster

Master of Pleasure

BACHELOR INTERNATIONAL:

Mister Temptation (Previously published as AMERICAN ASSHOLE)

Mister Irresistible

Mister Impossible

THE DATE DUO:

The Date Dare

The Date Deal

WALL STREET ROYALS:

FOK

Big Swinging D

All or None

THE BENEDICT BROTHERS

(Edited/rewritten version of Sons of Broad)

Perilous Kiss

Seductive Lies

Exposed Desire

OTHERS:

Madame President

Bucked

Her Last Hello

Altered Allies (currently unavailable)

*eNovella